PU

GHOSTS TI

A nightmarish mons
demonic boys with b.
children returning for revenge; bumps, squeaks and terror in the moonlight – all guaranteed to send a chill of fear up and down your spine.

Aidan Chambers well remembers being haunted when he was a boy. Three ugly-looking spectres hovered each night above a chest of drawers in his bedroom, never speaking. They never did him any harm either, they just stared, which was frightening enough. But ghosts need not always be horrific. Sometimes they can be very amusing as they land themselves, and the living people around them, in some peculiarly awkward situations!

Aidan Chambers has drawn together some of the best ghost stories ever written, all of which involve young people in some way – either haunting or haunted – and range from the truly terrifying to the downright funny. For readers of ten and over.

Jamie Hedges

1V

Mr O'shea.

GHOSTS THAT HAUNT YOU

Compiled by Aidan Chambers

Illustrated by Gareth Floyd

PUFFIN BOOKS

Puffin Books, Penguin Books Ltd, Harmondsworth, Middlesex, England
Penguin Books, 625 Madison Avenue, New York, New York 10022, U.S.A.
Penguin Books Australia Ltd, Ringwood, Victoria, Australia
Penguin Books Canada Ltd, 2801 John Street, Markham, Ontario, Canada L3R 1B4
Penguin Books (N.Z.) Ltd, 182–190 Wairau Road, Auckland 10, New Zealand

This selection first published by Kestrel Books 1980
Published in Puffin Books 1983

Made and printed in Great Britain by
Hazell Watson & Viney Ltd, Aylesbury, Bucks

Contents

Acknowledgements

The author and publishers would like to thank the following for their kind permission to use the stories included in this anthology: August Derleth for 'The Lonesome Place'; Pamela Hansford Johnson for 'The Empty Schoolroom'; R. Chetwynd-Hayes for 'Brownie'; Edward Arnold (Publishers) Ltd for 'Lost Hearts' by M. R. James; Joan Aitken for 'Tea at Ravensburgh' reprinted from *All and More* published by Jonathan Cape; 'School for the Unspeakable' reprinted by permission of the author and E. J. Carnell Literary Agency © 1937 by Popular Fiction Publishing Co. © 1973 by Carcosa; 'The Emissary' is reprinted by permission of Abner Stein and Harold Matson Company Inc. © 1947 Ray Bradbury © renewed 1975 by Ray Bradbury; Hughes Massie Ltd for 'The Lamp' by Agatha Christie; Brian Morse for 'We'll Always Have Tommy'; Macmillan, London and Basingstoke for 'Dead Trouble' by Aidan Chambers reprinted from *Ghosts 2*.

Foreword

When I was a boy, I was haunted for months by three ugly-looking spectres who hovered each night above a chest of drawers in my bedroom. They never spoke or did anything to harm me. They just stared. And that was frightening enough. Unwelcome guests; but since their nightmarish visitations I have enjoyed reading ghost stories.

When I became a professional author and began writing ghost stories as well as reading them, I was astonished to receive a steady flow of letters from young readers, both boys and girls, who wanted to tell me about the ghosts they believed they had seen – or heard or smelt or, most frightening of all, simply *felt*. What happened to me as a boy, it seems, was not unusual. A great many other people experience similar unnerving events.

Luckily there is a great difference between real-life ghosts and those that get into stories invented by authors. The real ones rarely harm anybody, the invented ones often do. Nevertheless, since so many boys and girls believe they have been haunted, I wondered why more writers didn't employ young people either as the haunters in their tales or as the haunted. (For there are quite as many family legends about ghostly boys and girls as there are about boys and girls being spooked.) So I started looking for stories that do involve young people in this way. *Ghosts That Haunt You* is a selection of the best.

I am glad to say that I think there is something for every ghost-story reader's taste. There are, for instance, weird apparitions that come and go without warning and have dire tales to tell; there are subtle and puzzling spirits that haunt their victims' minds rather than their bedrooms; there are sad and lonely wraiths that bother nobody, and there are some that seek to make life very unpleasant for any living person they can lay their cold ethereal hands upon. There are also a couple of humorous ghosts, a kind I especially enjoy but which you don't come across too often. In fact, they are so rare I had to write the story of one of them myself.

But in every story, whatever its kind, either the living ghost-seer or the ghost itself is a boy or a girl. The youngest is only just of school age; the oldest is eighteen and will never grow any older. I thank the authors of all of them for allowing me to include them here.

AIDAN CHAMBERS

The Lonesome Place

August Derleth

You who sit in your houses of nights, you who sit in the theatres, you who are gay at dances and parties – all you who are enclosed by four walls – you have no conception of what goes on outside in the dark. In the lonesome places. And there are so many of them, all over – in the country, in the small towns, in the cities. If you were out in the evenings, in the night, you would know about them, you would pass them and wonder, perhaps, and if you were a small boy you might be frightened. Frightened the way Johnny Newell and I were frightened, the way thousands of small boys from one end of the country to the other are being frightened when they have to go out alone at night, past lonesome places, dark and lightless, sombre and haunted . . .

I want you to understand that if it had not been for the lonesome place at the grain elevator, the place with the big old trees and the sheds up close to the pavement, and the piles of lumber – if it had not been for that place Johnny Newell and I would never have been guilty of murder. I say it even if there is nothing the law can do about it. They cannot touch us, but it is true, and I know, and Johnny knows, but we never talk about it, we never say anything. It is just something we keep here, behind our eyes, deep in our thoughts where it is a fact which is lost among thousands of others, but no less there, something we know beyond cavil.

It goes back a long way. But as time goes, perhaps it is not long. We were young, we were little boys in a small town. Johnny lived three houses away and across the street from me, and both of us lived in the block west of the grain elevator. We were never afraid to go past the lonesome place together. But we were not often together. Sometimes one of us had to go that way alone, sometimes the other. I went that way most of the time – there was no other, except to go far around, because that was the straight way down town, and I had to walk there, when my father was too tired to go.

In the evenings it would happen like this. My mother would discover that she had no sugar or salt or bologna, and she would say, 'Steve, you go down town and get it. Your father's too tired.'

I would say, 'I don't wanna.'

She would say, 'You go.'

I would say, 'I can go in the morning before school.'

She would say, 'You go now. I don't want to hear another word out of you. Here's the money.'

And I would have to go.

Going down was never quite so bad, because most of the time there was still some afterglow in the west, and a kind of pale light lay there, a luminousness, like part of the day lingering there, and all around town you could hear the kids hollering in the last hour they had to play, and you felt somehow not alone. You could go down into that dark place under the trees and you would never think of being lonesome. But when you came back – that was different.

When you came back the afterglow was gone; if the stars were out, you could never see them for the trees, and though the street lights were on – the old-fashioned lights arched over the crossroads – not a ray of them penetrated the lonesome place near to the elevator. There it was, half a block long, black as black could be, dark as the deepest night, with the shadows of the trees making it a solid place of darkness, with the faint glow of light where a street light pooled at the end of the street. Far away it seemed, and that other glow behind, where the other corner light lay.

And when you came that way you walked slower and slower. Behind you lay the brightly lit stores; all along the way there had been houses, with lights in the windows and music playing and voices of people sitting to talk on their porches. But up there, ahead of you, there was the lonesome place, with no house nearby, and up beyond it the tall, dark grain elevator, gaunt and forbidding. The lonesome place of trees and sheds and lumber, in which anything might be lurking, anything at all. The lonesome place where you were sure that something haunted the darkness waiting for the moment and the hour and the night when you came through to burst forth from its secret place and leap upon you, tearing you and rending you and doing the unmentionable things before it had done for you.

That was the lonesome place. By day it was oak and maple trees over a hundred years old, low enough so that you could almost touch the big spreading limbs; it was sheds and lumber piles which were seldom disturbed; it was a pavement and long grass, never mowed or kept down until late autumn, when somebody burned it off; it was a shady place in the hot summer days where some cool air always lingered.

You were never afraid of it by day, but by night it was a different place.

For, then, it was lonesome, away from sight or sound, a place of darkness and strangeness, a place of terror for little boys haunted by a thousand fears.

And every night, coming home from town, it happened like this. I would walk slower and slower, the closer I got to the lonesome place. I would think of every way around it. I would keep hoping somebody would come along, so that I could walk with him, Mr Newell, maybe, or old Mrs Potter, who lived farther up the street, or Reverend Bislor, who lived at the end of the block beyond the grain elevator. But nobody ever came. At this hour it was too soon after supper for them to go out, or, already out, too soon for them to return. So I walked slower and slower, until I got to the edge of the lonesome place – and then I ran as fast as I could, sometimes with my eyes closed.

Oh, I knew what was there, all right. I knew there was something in that dark, lonesome place. Perhaps it was the bogey-man. Sometimes my grandmother spoke of him, of how he waited in dark places for bad boys and girls. Perhaps it was an ogre. I knew about ogres in the books of fairy tales. Perhaps it was something else, something worse. I ran. I ran hard. Every blade of grass, every leaf, every twig that touched me was *its* hand reaching for me. The sound of my footsteps slapping the pavement were *its* steps pursuing. The hard breathing which was my own became *its* breathing in its frantic struggle to reach me, to rend and tear me, to imbue my soul with terror.

I would burst out of that place like a flurry of wind, fly

past the gaunt elevator, and not pause until I was safe in the yellow glow of the familiar street light. And then, in a few steps, I was home.

And mother would say, 'For the Lord's sake, have you been running on a hot night like this?'

I would say, 'I hurried.'

'You didn't have to hurry that much. I don't need it till breakfast time.'

And I would say, 'I coulda got it in the morning. I coulda run down before breakfast. Next time, that's what I'm gonna do.'

Nobody would pay any attention.

Some nights Johnny had to go down town, too. Things then weren't the way they are today, when every woman makes a ritual of afternoon shopping and seldom forgets anything.

In those days, they didn't go down town so often, and when they did, they had such lists they usually forgot something. And after Johnny and I had been through the lonesome place on the same night, we compared notes next day.

'Did you see anything?' he would ask.

'No, but I heard it,' I would say.

'I felt it,' he would whisper tensely. 'It's got big, flat clawed feet. You know what has got the ugliest feet around?'

'Sure, one of those stinking yellow soft-shell turtles.'

'It's got feet like that. Oh, ugly and soft, and sharp claws! I saw one out of the corner of my eye,' he would say.

'Did you see its face?' I would ask.

'It ain't got no face. Cross my heart an' hope to die, there ain't no face. That's worse'n if there was one.'

Oh, it was a horrible beast – not an animal, not a man – that lurked in the lonesome place and came forth predatorily at night, waiting there for us to pass. It grew like this, out of our mutual experiences. We discovered that it had scales, and a great long tail, like a dragon. It breathed from somewhere, hot as fire, but it had no face and no mouth in it, just a horrible opening in its throat. It was as big as an elephant, but it did not look like anything so friendly. It belonged there in the lonesome place; it would never go away; that was its home, and it had to wait for its food to come to it – the unwary boys and girls who had to pass through the lonesome place at night.

How I tried to keep from going near the lonesome place after dark!

'Why can't Mady go?' I would ask.

'Mady's too little,' Mother would answer.

'I'm not so big.'

'Oh, shush! You're a big boy now. Your Sears-Roebuck pants are long ones,' she would say.

'I don't care about any old Sears-Roebuck pants. I don't wanna go.'

'I want you to go. You never get up early enough in the morning.'

'But I will. I promise I will. I promise, Ma!' I would cry out.

'Tomorrow morning it will be a different story. No, you go.'

That was the way it went every time. I had to go. And Mady was the only one who guessed. 'Fraidycat,' she would whisper. Even she never really knew. She never had to go through the lonesome place after dark. They kept her at home. She never knew how something could lie up in those old trees, lie right along those old limbs across the pavement and drop down without a sound, clawing and tearing, something without a face, with ugly clawed feet like a soft-shell turtle's, with scales and a tail like a dragon, something as big as a horse, all black, like the darkness in that place.

But Johnny and I knew.

'It almost got me last night,' he would say, his voice low, looking anxiously out of the woodshed where we sat, as if *it* might hear us.

'Gee, I'm glad it didn't,' I would say. 'What was it like?'

'Big and black. Awful black. I looked around when I was running, and all of a sudden there wasn't any light way back at the other end. Then I knew it was coming. I ran like everything to get out of there. It was almost on me when I got away. Look there!'

And he would show me a rip in his shirt where a claw had come down.

'And you?' he would ask excitedly, big-eyed. 'What about you?'

'It was back behind the lumber piles when I came through,' I said. 'I could just feel it waiting. I was running, but it got right up – you look, there's a pile of lumber tipped over there.'

And we would walk down into the lonesome place at midday and look. Sure enough, there would be a pile of lumber tipped over, and we would look to where something had been lying down, the grass all pressed down. Sometimes we would find a handkerchief and wonder whether *it* had caught somebody.

Then we would go home and wait to hear if anyone was missing, speculating apprehensively all the way home whether *it* had got Mady or Christine or Helen, or any one of the girls in our class or Sunday School. Or whether maybe *it* had got Miss Doyle, the young primary grade teacher who had to walk that way sometimes after supper. But no one was ever reported missing, and the mystery grew. Maybe *it* had got some stranger who happened to be passing by and didn't know about the Thing that lived there in the lonesome place. We were sure *it* had got somebody.

'Some night I won't come back, you'll see,' I would say.

'Oh, don't be silly,' my mother would say.

What do grown-up people know about the things boys are afraid of? Oh, hickory switches and such like, they know that. But what about what goes on in their minds when they have to come home alone at night through the lonesome places? What do they know about lonesome places, where no light from the street corner ever comes? What do they know about a place and time when a boy is very small and very alone, and the night is as big as the town, and the darkness is the whole world? When grown-ups are big, old people who cannot understand anything, no matter how plain?

A boy looks up and out, but he can't look very far when the trees bend down over and press close, when the sheds rear up along one side and the trees on the other, when the darkness lies like a cloud along the pavement and the arc-lights are far, far away. No wonder, then, that Things grow in the darkness of lonesome places the way *it* grew in that dark place near the grain elevator. No wonder a boy runs like the wind until his heartbeats sound like a drum and push up to suffocate him.

'You're white as a sheet,' Mother would say sometimes. 'You've been running again.'

'You don't have to run,' my father would say. 'Take it easy.'

'I ran,' I would say. I wanted the worst way to say I had to run and to tell them why I had to. But I knew they wouldn't believe me any more than Johnny's parents believed him when he told them, as he did once.

He got a licking with a strap and had to go to bed.

I never got licked. I never told them.

But now it must be told, now it must be set down.

For a long time we forgot about the lonesome place. We grew older and we grew bigger. We went on through school into high school, and somehow we forgot about the Thing in the lonesome place. That place never changed. The trees grew older. Sometimes the lumber piles were bigger or smaller. Once the sheds were painted – red, like blood. Seeing them that way the first time, I remembered. Then I forgot again. We took to playing baseball and basketball and football. We began to swim in the river and to date the girls. We never talked about the Thing in the lonesome place any more, and when we went through there at night it was like something forgotten that lurked back in a corner of the mind. We thought of something we ought to remember, but never could quite remember; that was the way it seemed – like a memory locked away, far away in childhood. We never ran through that place, and sometimes it was even a good place to walk through with a girl, because she always snuggled up close and said how spooky it was there under the overhanging trees. But even then we never lingered there, not exactly lingered; we didn't run through there, but we walked without faltering or loitering, no matter how pretty a girl she was.

The years went past, and we never thought about the lonesome place again.

We never thought how there would be other little boys going through it at night, running with fast-beating hearts, breathless terror, anxious for the safety of the arclight beyond the margin of the shadow which confined the dweller in that place; the light-fearing creature that haunted the dark, like so many terrors swelling in similar lonesome places in the cities and small towns and countrysides all over the world, waiting to frighten little boys and girls, waiting to invade them with horror and unshakable fear – waiting for something more . . .

Three nights ago little Bobby Jeffers was killed in the lonesome place. He was all mauled and torn and partly crushed, as if something big had fallen on him. Johnny, who was on the Village Board, went to look at the place, and after he had been there, he telephoned me to go, too, before other people walked there.

I went down and saw the marks, too. It was just as the coroner said, only not an 'animal of some kind', as he put it. Something with a dragging tail, with scales, with great clawed feet – and I knew it had no face.

I knew, too, that Johnny and I were guilty. We had murdered Bobby Jeffers because the Thing that killed him was the Thing Johnny and I had created out of our childhood fears and left in that lonesome place to wait for some scared little boy at some minute in some hour during some dark night, a little boy who, like fat Bobby Jeffers, couldn't run as fast as Johnny and I could run.

And the worst is not that there is nothing to do, but that the lonesome place is being changed. The village is cutting down some of the trees now, removing the sheds, and putting up a street light in the middle of that place; it will not be dark and lonesome any longer, and the Thing that lives there will have to go somewhere else, where people are unsuspecting, to some other lonesome place in some other small town or city or countryside, where it will wait as it did here, for some frightened little boy or girl to come along, waiting in the dark and the lonesomeness . . .

The Empty Schoolroom

Pamela Hansford Johnson

My mother and father were in India and I had no aunts, uncles or cousins with whom I could spend my holidays; so I stayed behind in the drab and echoing school to amuse myself as best I could, my only companions the housekeeper, the maid, and Mademoiselle Fournier, who also had nowhere else to go.

Our school was just outside the village of Bellançay, which is in the north of France, four or five kilometres from Rouen. It was a tall, narrow house set upon the top of a hill, bare save for the great sweep of beech trees sheltering the long carriage drive. As I look back some twenty-seven years to my life there, it seems to me that the sun never shone, that the grass was always dun-coloured beneath a dun-coloured sky, and that the vast spaces of the lawns were broken perpetually by the scurry of dry brown leaves licked along by a small, bitter wind. This inaccurate impression remains with me because, I suppose, I was never happy at Bellançay. There were twenty or thirty other girls there – French, German or Swiss; I was the only English girl among them. Madame de Vallon, the headmistress, did not love my nation. She could not forget that she had been born in 1815, the year of defeat. With Mademoiselle Maury, the young assistant teacher, I was a little more at ease, for she, even if she did not care for me, had too volatile a nature not to smile and laugh sometimes, even for the benefit of those who were not her favourites.

Mademoiselle Fournier was a dependent cousin of our headmistress. She was in her late fifties, a little woman dry as a winter twig, her face very tight, small and wary under a wig of coarse yellow hair. To pay for her board and lodging she taught deportment; in her youth she had been at the Court of the Tsar, and it was said that at sixteen years of age she was betrothed to a Russian nobleman. There was some sort of mystery here, about which all the girls were curious. Louise de Chausson said her mother had told her the story – how the nobleman, on the eve of his wedding, had shot himself through the head, having received word that certain speculations in which he had for many years been involved had come to light, and that his arrest was imminent . . . 'And from that day,' Louise whispered, her prominent eyes gleaming in the candlelight, 'she began to wither and wither and wither away, till all her beauty was gone . . .' Yes, I can see Louise now, kneeling upon her bed at the end of the vast dormitory, her thick plait hanging down over her nightgown, the little cross with the turquoise glittering at her beautiful and grainy throat. The others believed the story implicitly, except the piece about Mademoiselle Fournier's lost beauty. That they could not stomach. No, she was ugly as a monkey and had always been so.

For myself, I disbelieved in the nobleman; believed in the beauty. I have always had a curious faculty for stripping age from a face, recognizing the structure of the bone and the original texture of the skin beneath the disguisings of blotch, red vein and loosened flesh. When I looked at

Mademoiselle Fournier I saw that the pinched and veinous nose had once been delicate and fine; that the sunken eyes had once been almond-shaped and blue; that the small, loose mouth had once pouted charmingly and opened upon romantic words. Why did I not believe in the nobleman? For no better reason than a distrust of Louise's information on any conceivable point. She was a terrible teller of falsehoods.

I was seventeen years old when I spent my last vacation at Bellançay, and knowing that my parents were to return to Europe in the following spring I watched the departure of the other girls with a heart not quite so heavy as was usual upon these occasions. In six months' time I, too, would be welcomed and loved, have adventures to relate and hopes upon which to feed.

I waved to them from a dormer window as they rattled away in fiacre and barouche down the drive between the beech trees, sired and damed, uncled and aunted, their boxes stacked high and their voices high as the treetops. They had never before seemed to me a particularly attractive group of girls – that is, not in the mass. There was, of course, Hélène de Courcey, with her great olive eyes; Madeleine Millet, whose pale red hair hung to her knees; but in the cluster they had no particular charm. That day, however, as, in new bonnets flowered and feathered and gauzed, they passed from sight down the narrowing file of beeches, I thought them all beautiful as princesses, and as princesses fortunate. Perhaps the nip in the air of a grey June made their cheeks rose-red, their eyes bright as the eyes of desirable young ladies in ballrooms.

The last carriage disappeared, the last sound died away.

I turned from the window and went down the echoing stairs, flight after flight to the *salle à manger*, where my luncheon awaited me.

I ate alone. Mademoiselle Fournier took her meals in her own room upon the second floor, reading as she ate, crumbs falling from her lip on to the page. Tonight she and I, in the pattern of all holiday nights, would sit together for a while in the drawing room before retiring.

'You don't make much of a meal, I must say,' Marie, the maid, rebuked me, as she cleared the plates. 'You can't afford to grow thinner, Mademoiselle, or you'll snap in two.' She brought me some cherries, which I would not eat then but preferred to take out with me in the garden. 'I'll wrap them up for you. No! you can't put them in your handkerchief like that; you'll stain it.'

She chattered to me for a while, in her good nature trying to ease my loneliness. Marie, at least, had relations in the village with whom she sometimes spent her evenings. 'What are you going to do with yourself, eh? Read your eyes out as usual?'

'I shall walk this afternoon, unless I find it too chilly.'

'You'll find it raining,' said Marie, cocking a calculating eye towards the high windows, 'in an hour. No, less; in half an hour.'

She busied herself wrapping up my cherries, which she handed to me in a neat parcel with a firm finger-loop of string. 'If it's wet you can play the piano.'

'You've forgotten,' I said, 'we have none now, or shan't have till they send the new one.'

Madame de Vallon had recently sold the old instrument, ugly and tinny, and with the money from the sale plus some money raised by parents' subscription had bought a grand pianoforte from Monsieur Oury, the mayor, whose eldest daughter, the musical one, had lately died.

'You can play on Mademoiselle Fournier's,' said Marie, 'she won't mind. You go and ask her.'

'What, is there another piano in the school?' I was amazed. I had been at Bellançay for seven years and had fancied no corner of the building unknown to me.

'Ah-ha,' said Marie triumphantly, 'there are still things you don't know, eh? You don't have to do the housework, or you'd be wiser.'

'But where is it?'

'In the empty schoolroom.'

I laughed at her. 'But they're all empty now! Whatever do you mean?'

'The one at the top,' she said impatiently, 'the one up the little flight of four stairs.'

'But that's the lumber room!'

'There's lumber in it. But it was a schoolroom once. It was when my aunt worked here. The piano's up there still, though *she* never plays it now.' Marie jerked her head skywards to indicate Mademoiselle Fournier upstairs.

I was fascinated by this information. We girls had never entered the lumber room because no attraction had been attached to it: to us it was simply a small, grimy door in the attic, locked we imagined, as we had never seen anyone go in or out. All we knew was that old books, valises, crates of unwanted china, were sometimes stacked up there out of the way.

There! I have failed to make my point quite clear. I must try again. *There was no mystery whatsoever attaching to this room*, which is the reason why no girl had ever tried the handle. Schoolgirls are curious and roaming creatures; how better can they be kept from a certain path than by the positive assurance that it is a *cul-de-sac*?

Dismissing Marie, I determined to go and seek permission from Mademoiselle Fournier to play upon her pianoforte. Since the departure of the old one, I had missed my music lessons and above all my practising; most of the girls were delighted to be saved a labour which to me, though I was an indifferent performer, had never been anything but a pleasure.

Mademoiselle had finished her meal and was just coming out upon the landing as I ran up the stairs to find her. I made my request.

She looked at me. 'Who told you about the instrument?'

'Marie.'

She was silent. Her brows moved up and down, moving the wig as they did so. It was a familiar trick with her when she was puzzled or annoyed. At last she said, without expression, 'No, you may not go up there,' and pushing me, hurried on downstairs.

At the turn of the staircase, however, she stopped and looked up. Her whole face was working with some unrecognizable emotion and her cheeks were burning red. 'Is there *no* place one can keep to oneself?' she cried at me furiously, and ducking her head, ran on.

When we sat that evening in the drawing room, in our chairs turned to the fireless grate, she made no reference to the little scene of that afternoon. I thought she was, perhaps, sorry for having spoken so sharply: for she asked me a few personal questions of a kindly nature and just before bedtime brought out a tin box full of sugared almonds, which she shared with me.

She rose a little before I did, leaving me to retire when I chose. I stayed for perhaps half an hour in that vast, pale room with its moth-coloured draperies and its two tarnished chandeliers hanging a great way below the ceiling. Then I took up my candle and went to bed.

Now I must insist that I was a docile girl, a little sullen, perhaps, out of an unrealized resentment against my parents for (as I thought) deserting me; but obedient. I never had a bad conduct report from any of our teachers. It is important that this fact should be realized, so the reader shall know that what I did was not of my own free will.

I could not sleep. I lay open-eyed until my candle burned halfway down and the moon shifted round into the window-pane, weaving the golden light with its own blue-silver. I had no thought of any importance. Small pictures from the day's humdrum events flashed across my brain. I saw the neatly-looped parcel of cherries, the currant stain at the hem of Marie's apron, the starch-blue bird on the bonnet of Louise de Chausson, who had left Bellançay to marry an elderly and not very rich nobleman of Provence. I saw the leaves scurrying over the grey lawns, saw a woodpecker rapping at the trunk of the tree behind the house. What I did not see was the face of Mademoiselle Fournier upturned from thc stairway. She never entered my thoughts at all.

And so it is very strange that just before dawn I rose up, put on my dressing gown and sought about the room until I found a pair of gloves my father had had made for me in India, fawn-coloured, curiously stitched in gold and dark green thread. These I took up, left the room and made my way silently up through the quiet house till I came to the door of the lumber room – or, as Marie had called it, the empty schoolroom. I paused with my hand upon the latch and listened. There was no sound except the impalpable breathing of the night, compound perhaps of the breathings of all who sleep, or perhaps of the movement of the moon through the gathered clouds.

I raised the latch gently and stepped within the room, closing the door softly behind me.

The chamber ran halfway across the length of the house at the rear of it, and was lighted by a ceiling window through which the moonrays poured lavishly down. It was still a schoolroom, despite the lumber stacked at the far end, the upright piano standing just behind the door. Facing me was a dais, on which stood a table and a chair. Before the dais were row upon row of desks, with benches behind. Everything was very dusty. With my finger I wrote DUST upon the teacher's table, then scuffed the word out again.

I went to the pianoforte. Behind the lattice-work was a ruching of torn red silk; the candle stumps in the sconces were red also. On the rack stood a piece of music, a Chopin nocturne simplified for beginners.

Gingerly I raised the lid and a mottled spider ran across the keys, dropped on hasty thread to the floor and ran away. The underside of the lid was completely netted by his silk; broken strands waved in the disturbed air and over the discoloured keys. As a rule I am afraid of spiders. That night I was not afraid. I laid my gloves on the keyboard, then closed the piano lid upon them.

I was ready to go downstairs. I took one glance about the room and for a moment thought I saw a shadowy form sitting upon one of the back benches, a form that seemed to weep. Then the impression passed away, and there was only the moonlight painting the room with its majesty. I went out, latched the door and crept back to my bed where, in the first colouring of dawn, I fell asleep.

Next day it was fine. I walked to the river in the morning, and in the afternoon worked at my *petit-point* upon the terrace. At teatime an invitation came for me. The mayor, Monsieur Oury, wrote to Mademoiselle Fournier saying he believed there was a young lady left behind at school for the holidays, and that if she would care to dine at his house upon the following evening it would be a great pleasure to him and to his two young daughters. 'We are not a gay house these days,' he wrote, 'but if the young lady cares for books and flowers there are a great number of both in my library and conservatory.'

'Shall I go?' I asked her.

'But of course! It is really a great honour for you. Do you know who the mayor's mother was before her marriage? She was a Uzès. Yes. And when she married Monsieur Oury's father, a very handsome man, her family cut her off with nothing at all and never spoke to her again. But they were very happy. You must wear your best gown and your white hat. Take the gown to Marie and she will iron it for you.'

The day upon which I was to visit Monsieur Oury was sunless and chilly. Plainly the blue dress that Marie had so beautifully spotted and pressed would not do at all. I had, however, a gown of fawn-coloured merino, plain but stylish, with which my brown straw hat would look very well.

Mademoiselle Fournier left the house at four o'clock to take tea with the village priest. She looked me over before she went, pinched my dress, tweaked it, pulled out the folds, and told me to sit quite still until the mayor's carriage came for me at half past six. 'Sit like a mouse, mind, or you will spoil the effect. Remember, Monsieur Oury is not nobody.' She said suddenly, 'Where are your gloves?'

I had forgotten them.

'Forgetting the very things that make a lady look a lady! Go and fetch them at once. Marie!'

The maid came in.

'Marie, see Mademoiselle's gloves are nice, and brush her down once more just as you see the carriage enter the drive. I mustn't wait now. Well, Maud, I wish you a pleasant evening. Don't forget you must be a credit to us.'

When she had gone Marie asked for my gloves. 'You'd better wear your brown ones with that hat, Mademoiselle.'

'Oh!' I exclaimed, 'I can't! I lost one of them on the expedition last week.'

'Your black, then?'

'They won't do. They'd look dreadful with this gown and hat. I know! I have a beautiful Indian pair that will match my dress exactly! I'll go and look for them.'

I searched. The reader must believe that I hunted all over my room for them anxiously, one eye upon the clock, though it was not yet twenty minutes past four. Chagrined, really upset at the thought of having my toilette ruined, I sat down upon the edge of the bed and began to cry a little. Tears came very easily to me in those lost and desolate days.

From high up in the house I heard a few notes of the piano, the melody of a Chopin nocturne played fumblingly in the treble, and I thought at once, 'Of course! The gloves are up there, where I hid them.'

The body warns us of evil before the senses are half awakened. I knew no fear as I ran lightly up towards the empty schoolroom, yet as I reached the door I felt a wave of heat engulf me, and knew a sick, nauseous stirring within my body. The notes, audible only to my ear (not to Marie's, for even at that moment I could hear her calling out some inquiry or gossip to the housekeeper), ceased. I lifted the latch and looked in.

The room appeared to be deserted, yet I could see the presence within it and know its distress. I peeped behind the door.

At the piano sat a terribly ugly, thin young girl in a dunce's cap. She was half turned towards me, and I saw her pig-like profile, the protruding teeth, the spurt of sandy eyelash. She wore a holland dress in the fashion of twenty years ago, and lean yellow streamers of hair fell down over her back from beneath the paper cone. Her hands, still resting on the fouled keyboard, were meshed about with the spider's web; beneath them lay my Indian gloves.

I made a movement towards the girl. She swivelled sharply and looked me full in the face. Her eyes were all white, red-rimmed, but tearless.

To get my gloves I must risk touching her. We looked at each other, she and I, and her head shrank low between her hunching shoulders. Somehow I must speak to her friendlily, disarm her while I gained my objective.

'Was it you playing?' I asked.

No answer. I closed my eyes. Stretching out my hands as in a game of blind man's buff, I sought for the keyboard.

'I have never heard you before,' I said.

I touched something: I did not know whether it was a glove or her dead hand.

'Have you been learning long?' I said. I opened my eyes. She was gone. I took my gloves, dusted off the webs and ran, ran so fast down the well of the house that on the last flight I stumbled and fell breathless into Marie's arms.

'Oh, I have had a fright! I have had a fright!'

She led me into the drawing room, made me lie down, brought me a glass of wine.

'What is it, Mademoiselle? Shall I fetch the housekeeper? What has happened?'

But the first sip of wine had made me wary. 'I thought I saw someone hiding in my bedroom, a man. Perhaps a thief.'

At this the house was roused. Marie, the housekeeper and the gardener, who had not yet finished his work, searched every room (the lumber room, too, I think) but found nothing. I was scolded, petted, dosed, and Marie insisted, when the housekeeper was out of the way, on a *soupçon* of rouge on my cheeks because, she said, I could not upset Monsieur le Maire by looking like a dead body – he, poor man, having so recently had death in his house!

I recovered myself sufficiently to climb into the carriage, when it came, to comport myself decently on the drive, and to greet the mayor and his two daughters with dignity. Dinner, however, was a nightmare. My mind was so full of the horror I had seen that I could not eat – indeed I could barely force my trembling hand to carry the fork to my lips.

The mayor's daughters were only children, eleven and thirteen years old. At eight o'clock he bade them say good night to me and prepare for bed. When they had left us I told him I thought I had stayed long enough: but with a very grave look he placed his hand upon my arm and pressed me gently back into my chair.

'My dear young lady,' he said, 'I know your history, I know you are lonely and unhappy in France without your parents. Also I know that you have suffered some violent shock. Will you tell me about it and let me help you?'

The relief of his words, of his wise and kindly gaze, was too much for me. For the first time in seven years I felt fathered and in haven. I broke down and cried tempestuously, and he did not touch me or speak to me till I was a little more calm. Then he rang for the servant and told her to bring some lime-flower tea. When I had drunk and eaten some of the sweet cake that he urged upon me I told him about the empty schoolroom and of the horror which sat there at the webbed piano.

When I had done he was silent for a little while. Then he took both my hands in his.

'Mademoiselle,' he said, 'I am not going to blame you for the sin of curiosity; I think there was some strange compulsion upon you to act as you did. Therefore I mean to shed a little light upon this sad schoolroom by telling you the story of Mademoiselle Fournier.'

I started.

'No,' he continued restrainingly, 'you must listen quietly; and what I tell you you must never repeat to a soul save your own mother until both Mademoiselle Fournier and Madame de Vallon, her cousin, have passed away.'

I have kept this promise. They have been dead some fourteen years.

Monsieur Oury settled back in his chair. A tiny but comforting fire was lit in the grate, and the light of it was like a ring of guardian angels about us.

'Mademoiselle Fournier,' he began, 'was a very beautiful and proud young woman. Although she had no dowry, she was yet considered something of a *partie*, and in her nineteenth year she became affianced to a young Russian nobleman who at that time was living with his family upon an estate near Arles. His mother was not too pleased with the match, but she was a good woman, and she treated Charlotte – that is, Mademoiselle Fournier – with kindness. Just before the marriage Charlotte's father, who had been created a marquis by Bonaparte and now, by tolerance, held a minor government post under Louis Philippe, was found to have embezzled many thousands of francs.'

'Her father!' I could not help but exclaim.

Monsieur Oury smiled wryly. 'Legend has the lover for villain, eh? No; it was Aristide Fournier, a weak man, unable to stomach any recession in his fortunes. Monsieur Fournier shot himself as the gendarmes were on their way to take him. Charlotte, her marriage prospects destroyed, came near to lunacy. When she recovered from her long illness her beauty had gone. The mother of her ex-fiancé, in pity, suggested that a friend of hers, a lady at the Court of the Tsar, should employ Charlotte as governess to her children, and in Russia Charlotte spent nine years. She returned to France to assist her cousin with the school at Bellançay that Madame de Vallon had recently established.'

'Why did she return?' I said, less because I wished to know the answer than because I wished to break out of the veil of the past he was drawing about us both, and to feel myself a reality once more, Maud Arlett, aged seventeen years and nine months, brown hair and grey eyes, five foot seven and a half inches tall.

I did not succeed. The veil tightened, grew more opaque. 'Nobody knows. There were rumours. It seems not improbable that she was dismissed by her employer . . . why, I don't know. It is an obscure period in Charlotte's history.'

He paused, to pour more tea for me.

'It was thought at first that Charlotte would be of great assistance to Madame de Vallon, teach all subjects and act as Madame's secretary. It transpired, however, that Charlotte was nervous to the point of sickness, and that she would grow less and less capable of teaching young girls. Soon she had no duties in the school except to give lessons in music and deportment.

'The music room was in the attic, which was then used as a schoolroom also. The pianoforte was Charlotte's own, one of the few things saved from the wreck of her home.'

Monsieur Oury rose and walked out of the ring of firelight. He stood gazing out of the window, now beaded by a thin rain, and his voice grew out of the dusk as the music of waves grows out of the sea. 'I shall tell you the rest briefly, Mademoiselle. It distresses me to tell it to you at all, but I think I can help you in no other way.

'A young girl came to the school, a child; perhaps twelve or thirteen years of age. Her mother and father were in the East, and she was left alone, even during the vacations –'

'Like myself!' I cried.

'Yes, like yourself; and I have an idea that that is why she chose you for her ... *confidante*.'

I shuddered.

He seemed to guess at my movement for, turning from the window, he returned to the firelight and to me.

'In one way, however, she was unlike you as can possibly be imagined, Mademoiselle.' He smiled with a faint, sad gallantry. 'She was exceedingly ugly.

'From the first, Charlotte took a dislike to her, and it grew to mania. The child, Thérèse Dasquier, was never very intelligent; in Charlotte's grip she became almost imbecile. Charlotte was always devising new punishments, new humiliations. Thérèse became the mock and the pity of the school.'

'But Madame de Vallon, couldn't she have stopped it?' I interrupted indignantly.

'My dear,' Monsieur Oury replied sadly, 'like many women of intellect – she is, as you know, a fine teacher – she is blind to most human distress. She is, herself, a kind woman: she believes others are equally kind, cannot believe there could be . . . suffering . . . torment . . . going on beneath her very nose. Has she ever realized *your* loneliness, Mademoiselle, given you any motherly word, or . . . ? I thought not. But I am digressing, and that I must not do. We have talked too much already.

'One night Thérèse Dasquier arose quietly, crept from the dormitory and walked barefooted a mile and a half in the rain across the fields to the river, where she drowned herself.'

'Oh, God,' I murmured, my heart cold and heavy as a stone.

'God, I think,' said Monsieur Oury, 'cannot have been attentive at that time . . .' His face changed. He added hastily, 'And God forgive me for judging Him. We cannot know – we cannot guess . . .' he continued rapidly, in a dry, rather high voice oddly unlike his own. 'There was scandal, great scandal. Thérèse's parents returned to France and everyone expected them to force the truth to light. They turned out to be frivolous and selfish people, who could scarcely make even a parade of grief for a child they had never desired and whose death they could not regret.

Thérèse was buried and forgotten. Slowly, very slowly, the story also was forgotten. After all, nobody *knew* the truth, they could only make conjecture.'

'Then how did you know?' I cried out.

'Because Madame de Vallon came to me in bitter distress with the tale of the rumours and besought me to clear Charlotte's name. You see, she simply could not believe a word against her. And at the same time the aunt of Marie, the maid, came to me swearing she could prove the truth of the accusations ... Three days afterwards she was killed in the fire which destroyed the old quarter of Bellançay.'

I looked my inquiry into his face.

'I knew which of the women spoke the truth,' he replied, answering me, 'because in Madame de Vallon's face I saw concern for her own blood. In the other woman's I saw concern for a child who to her was nothing.'

'But still, you *guessed*!' I protested.

He turned upon me his long and grave regard. 'You,' he said, '*you* do not know the truth? Even you?'

I do not know how I endured the following weeks in that lonely school. I remember how long I lay shivering in my bed, staring into the flame of the candle because I felt that in the brightest part of it alone was refuge, how the sweat jumped out from my brow at the least sound in the stillness of midnight, and how, towards morning, I would fall into some morose and terrible dream of dark stairways and locked doors.

Yet, as day by day, night by night, went by with no untoward happening, my spirit knew some degree of easing and I began once more to find comfort in prayer – that is, I dared once again to cover my face while I repeated 'Our

Father', and to rise from my knees without fear of what might be standing patiently at my shoulder.

The holidays drew to an end. 'Tomorrow,' said Mademoiselle Fournier, folding her needlework in preparation for bed, 'your companions will be back with you once more. You'll like that, eh?'

Ever since my request and her refusal, she had been perfectly normal in her manner – I mean, she had been normally sour, polite, withdrawn.

'I shall like it,' I sighed, 'only too well.'

She smiled remotely. 'I am not a lively companion for you, Maud, I fear. Still, I am as I am. I am too old to change myself.'

She went on upstairs, myself following, our candles smoking in the draught and our shadows prancing upon the wall.

I said my prayers and read for a little while. I was unusually calm, feeling safety so nearly within my reach that I need be in no hurry to stretch out my hand and grasp it tight. The bed seemed softer than usual, the sheets sweet-smelling, delicately warm and light. I fell into a dreamless sleep.

I awoke suddenly to find the moon full on my face. I sat up, dazzled by her light, a strange feeling of energy tingling in my body. 'What is it,' I whispered, 'that I must do?'

The moon shone broadly on the great surfaces of gleaming wood, on the bureau, the tallboy, the wardrobe, flashed upon the mirror, sparkled on the spiralling bedposts. I slipped out of bed and in my nightgown went out into the passage.

It was very bright and still. Below me, the stairs fell steeply to the tessellated entrance hall. To my right the passage narrowed to the door behind which Mademoiselle Fournier slept, her wig upon a candlestick, her book and her spectacles lying on the rug at her side – so Marie had described her to me. Before me the stairs rose to the turn of the landing, from which a further flight led to the second floor, the third floor and the attics. The wall above the stair rail was white with the moon.

I felt the terror creeping up beneath my calm, though only as one might feel the shadow of pain while in the grip of a drug. I was waiting now as I had been instructed to wait, and I knew for what. I stared upwards, my gaze fastened upon the turn of the stairs.

Then, upon the moonlit wall, there appeared the shadow of a cone.

She stood just out of sight, her fool's-capped head nodding forward, listening even as I was listening.

I held my breath. My forehead was ice-cold.

She came into view then, stepping carefully, one hand upholding a corner of her skirt, the other feeling its way along the wall. As she reached me I closed my eyes. I felt her pass by, knew she had gone along the passage to the room of Mademoiselle Fournier. I heard a door quietly opened and shut.

In those last moments of waiting my fear left me, though I could move neither hand nor foot. My ears were sharp for the least sound.

It came: a low and awful cry, tearing through the quiet of the house and blackening the moonlight itself. The door opened again.

She came hastening out, and in the shadow of the cap she smiled. She ran on tiptoe past me, up the stairs.

The last sound? I thought it had been the death cry of Mademoiselle Fournier; but there was yet another.

As Marie and the housekeeper came racing down, white-faced, from their rooms (they must have passed her as she stood in the shade) I heard very distinctly the piping voice of a young girl:

'*Tiens, Mademoiselle, je vous remercie beaucoup!*'

We went together, Marie, the housekeeper and I, into the room of Charlotte Fournier, and only I did not cry out when we looked upon the face.

'You see,' said Monsieur Oury, on the day I left Bellançay for ever to join my parents in Paris, 'she did make you her *confidante*. She gave to you the privilege of telling her story and publishing her revenge. Are you afraid of her now, knowing that there was no harm in her for *you*, knowing that she has gone for ever, to trouble no house again?'

'I am not afraid,' I said, and I believed it was true; but even now I cannot endure to awaken suddenly on moonlit nights, and I fling my arms about my husband and beg him to rouse up and speak with me until the dawn.

Brownie

R. Chetwynd-Hayes

The house was built of grey stone, and stood on the edge of a vast moor; an awesome, desolate place, where the wind roared across a sea of heather and screamed like an army of lost souls.

Our father drove into a muddy, weed-infested drive, then braked to a halt. He smiled over his shoulder at Rodney and me, then said cheerfully: 'You'll be very happy here.'

We had grave doubts. On closer inspection the stonework was very dirty, the paintwork was flaking, and generally the house looked as unrelenting as the moor that lay beyond. Father opened the door and got out, his face set in that determinedly cheerful expression parents assume whenever they wish to pretend that all is well, even though appearances suggest otherwise.

'Fine people, Mr and Mrs Fairweather.' He gripped Rodney's arm, then mine, and guided us up a flight of stone steps towards a vast, oak door. 'You'll love 'em. Then, there are all those lovely moors for you to play on. Wish I was staying with you, instead of going back to India. But duty calls.'

He was lying, we both knew it, and perhaps the knowledge made parting all the more sad. He raised a bronzed hand, but before he could grasp the knocker, the door creaked open and there stood Mrs Fairweather.

'Major Sinclair.' She stood to one side for us to enter. 'Come in, Sir, and the young 'uns. The wind's like a knife, and cuts a body to the bone.'

The hall was large, bare, lined with age-darkened oak panels; doors broke both walls on either side of a massive staircase, and there was an old, churchy smell.

'Come into the kitchen with you,' Mrs Fairweather commanded, 'that being the only room that's livable in on the ground floor. The rest is locked up.'

The kitchen lay behind the staircase; a grandfather of all kitchens, having a red tiled floor, a spluttering iron range that positively shone from frequent applications of black lead, and an array of gleaming copper saucepans hanging on brass hooks over the mantelpiece.

A tall, lean old man was seated behind a much-scrubbed deal table. He rose as we entered, revealing that he wore a dark-blue boiler suit and a checked cloth cap.

'Fairweather,' his wife snapped, 'where's yer manners? Take yer cap off.'

Mr Fairweather reluctantly, or so it appeared to me, took off his cap, muttered some indistinguishable words, then sat down again. Mrs Fairweather turned to Father.

'You mustn't mind him, Sir. He's not used to company, but he's got a heart. I'll say that for him. Now, Sir, is there anything you'd like to settle with me before you leave?'

'No,' Father was clearly dying to be off. 'The extra sum we agreed upon will be paid by Simpson & Brown on the first of every month. The girl I engaged as governess will arrive tomorrow. Let me see,' he consulted a notebook, 'Miss Rose Fortesque.' He put the notebook away. 'I think that's all.'

'Right you are, Sir,' Mrs Fairweather nodded her grey head. 'I expect you'll want to say a few words to the little fellows before you leave, so me and Fairweather will make ourselves scarce. Fairweather . . .' The old man raised his head. 'Come on, we'll make sure the chicken are bedded down.'

Mr Fairweather followed her out through the kitchen doorway, muttering bad temperedly, and we were left alone with Father, who was betraying every sign of acute discomfort.

'Well, boys,' he was still determined to appear cheerful, 'I guess this is good-bye. You know I'd have loved to have taken you with me, but India is no place for growing boys, and now your mother has passed on there'd be no one to look after you. You'll be comfortable enough here, and Miss Fortesque will teach you all you need to know before you go to school next autumn. O.K.?'

I felt like choking, but Rodney, who had a far less emotional nature, was more prepared to deal with events of the moment.

'Do we own this house, Father?'

'I own this house,' Father corrected gently, 'and no doubt you will one day. As I told you, Mr and Mrs Fairweather are only caretakers, and they are allowed to cultivate some of the ground for their own use. Back before the days of Henry the Eighth, the house was a monastery, but since the Reformation it's been a private house. Your great uncle Charles was the last of our family to live here. I've never found the time to bring the old place up to scratch, so it has stood empty, save for the Fairweathers, since he died.'

'Pity,' said Rodney.

'Quite,' Father cleared his throat. 'Well, I expect the old . . . Mrs Fairweather has a good hot meal waiting for you, so I'll push off.' He bent down and kissed us lightly on the foreheads, then walked briskly to the kitchen door. 'Mrs Fairweather, I'm off.'

The speed with which the old couple reappeared suggested the chicken must be bedded down in the hall. Mr Fairweather made straight for his seat behind the table, while his wife creased her stern face into a polite smile.

'So you'll be going, Sir. I hope it won't be too long before we see you again.'

'No indeed.' Father shook her hand, his expression suddenly grave. 'No time at all. 'Bye, boys, do what the good Mrs Fairweather tells you. Good-bye, Fairweather.' He could not resist a bad joke. 'Hope it keeps fine for you.'

The old man half rose, grunted, then sat down again. Mrs Fairweather preceded Father into the hall. We heard the front door open, then the sound of Father's car; the crunch of gravel as he drove away. He was gone. We never saw him again. He was killed on the Indian North West Frontier fighting Afghanistan tribesmen, and, had he been consulted, I am certain that is the way he would have preferred to die. He was, above all, a soldier.

As Mrs Fairweather never failed to stress, food at Sinclair Abbey was plain, but good. We ate well, worked hard, for Mr Fairweather saw no reason why two extra pairs of hands should not be put to gainful employment, and above all, we played. An old, almost empty house is an ideal playground for two boys. The unused rooms, whenever we could persuade Mrs Fairweather to unlock the doors, were a particular joy. Dust-shrouded furniture crouched like beasts of prey against walls on which the paper had long since died. In the great dining room were traces of the old refectory where medieval monks had dined before Henry's henchmen had cast them out. One stained-glass window, depicting Abraham offering up Isaac as a sacrifice, could still be seen through a veil of cobwebs; an oak, high-backed chair, surmounted by a crucifix, suggested it had once been the property of a proud abbot. For young, inquiring eyes, remains of the old monastery could still be found.

Rose Fortesque came, as Father had promised, the day after our arrival. Had we been ten years older, doubtless we would have considered her to be a slim, extremely pretty, if somewhat retiring girl. As it was, we found her a great disappointment. Her pale, oval face, enhanced by a pair of rather sad blue eyes, gave the impression she was always on the verge of being frightened, the result possibly of being painfully shy.

Where Father had found her I have not the slightest idea. More than likely at some teachers' agency, or wherever prospective governesses parade their scholastic wares, but of a certainty, she was not equipped to deal with two high-spirited boys. It took but a single morning for us to become aware of this fact, and with the cruelty of unthinking youth, we took full advantage of the situation. She was very frightened after finding a frog in her bed, and a grass snake in her handbag, and from then onwards, she watched us with sad, reproachful eyes.

It was fully seven days after our arrival at Sinclair Abbey when we first met Brownie. Our bedroom was way up under the eaves, a long, barren room, furnished only by our two beds, a wardrobe, and two chairs, Mrs Fairweather having decided mere boys required little else. There was no electricity in that part of the house. A single candle lit us to bed, and once that was extinguished, there was only the pale rectangle of a dormer window which, in the small hours, when the sky was clear, allowed the moon to bathe the room in a soft, silver glow.

I woke suddenly, and heard the clock over the old stables strike two. It was a clear, frosty night, and a full moon stared in through the window, so that all the shadows had been chased into hiding behind the wardrobe, under the beds, and on either side of the window. Rodney was snoring, and I was just considering the possibility of throwing a boot at him, when I became aware there was a third presence in the room. I raised my head from the pillow. A man dressed in a monk's robe was sitting on the foot of my bed. The funny thing was, I couldn't feel his weight, and I should have done so, because my feet appeared to be underneath him.

I sat up, but he did not move, only continued to sit motionless, staring at the left-hand wall. The cowl of his robe was flung back to reveal a round, dark-skinned face, surmounted by a fringe of black curly hair surrounding a bald patch that I seemed to remember was called a tonsure. I was frightened, but pretended I wasn't. I whispered:

'Who are you? What do you want?'

The monk neither answered nor moved, so I tried again, this time a little louder.

'What are you doing here?'

He continued to sit like a figure in a wax museum, so I decided to wake Rodney – no mean task for he slept like Rip van Winkle. My second shoe did the trick and he woke protesting loudly:

'Wassat? Young Harry, I'll do you.'

'There's a man sitting on the foot of my bed, and he won't move.'

'What!' Rodney sat up, rubbed his eyes, then stared at our silent visitor. 'Who is he?'

'I don't know. I've asked him several times, but he doesn't seem to hear.'

'Perhaps he's asleep.'

'His eyes are open.'

'Well,' Rodney took a firm grip of my shoe, 'we'll soon find out.' And he hurled the shoe straight at the brown-clad figure.

Neither of us really believed what our eyes reported: the shoe went right through the tonsured head and landed with a resounding smack on a window-pane. But still there was no response from the monk, and now I was so frightened my teeth were chattering.

'I'm going to fetch Mrs Fairweather,' Rodney said after a while, 'she'll know what to do.'

'Rodney,' I swallowed, 'you're not going to leave me alone with – him, are you?'

Rodney was climbing out of the far side of the bed.

'He won't hurt you, he doesn't move, and if he does you can belt under the bed. I say, chuck the candle over, and the matches, I've got to find my way down to the next floor.'

Left alone, I studied our visitor with a little more attention than formerly, for, as he appeared to be harmless, my fear was gradually subsiding.

I knew very little about monks, but this one seemed to be a rather shabby specimen; his gown was old, and there was even a small hole in one sleeve, as if he indulged in the bad habit of leaning his elbows on the table. Furthermore, on closer inspection – and by now I had summoned up enough courage to crawl forward a short way along the bed – he was in need of a shave. There was a distinct stubble on his chin, and one hand, that rested on his knee, had dirt under the finger-nails. Altogether, I decided, this was a very scruffy monk.

Rodney had succeeded in waking the Fairweathers. The old lady could be heard protesting loudly at being disturbed, and an occasional rumble proclaimed that Mr Fairweather was not exactly singing for joy. Slippered feet came padding up the stairs, and now Mrs Fairweather's unbroken tirade took on recognizable words.

'I won't have him lurking around the place. It's more than I'm prepared to stand, though why two lumps of boys couldn't have chased him out, without waking a respectable body from her well-earned sleep, I'll never know.'

'But he doesn't move,' Rodney's voice intervened.

'I'll move him.'

She came in through the doorway like a gust of wind, a bundle of fury wrapped in a flowered dressing gown, and in one hand she carried a striped bath towel.

'Get along with you.' She might have been shooing off a stray cat. 'I won't have you lurking around the house. Go on – out.'

The words had no effect, but the bath towel did. Mrs Fairweather waved it in, or rather through, the apparition's face. The figure stirred, rather like a clockwork doll making a first spasmodic move, then the head turned and a look of deep distress appeared on the up to now emotionless face. The old lady continued to scold, and flapped the towel even more vigorously.

'Go on, if I've told you once, I've told you a hundred times, you're not to bother respectable folk. Go where you belong.'

The monk flowed into an upright position; there is no other word to describe the action. Then he began to dance in slow motion towards the left-hand wall, Mrs Fairweather pursuing him with her flapping towel. It was a most awesome sight; first the left leg came very slowly upwards, and seemed to find some invisible foothold, then the right drifted past it, while both arms gently clawed the air. It took the monk some three minutes to reach the left-hand wall; a dreadful, slow, macabre dance, performed two feet above floor level, with an irate Mrs Fairweather urging him on with her flapping towel, reinforced by repeated instructions to go, and not come back, while her husband, ludicrous in a white flannel nightgown, watched sardonically from the doorway.

The monk at last came to the wall. His left leg went through it, then his right arm, followed by his entire body.

The last we saw of him was the heel of one sandal, which had a broken strap. Mrs Fairweather folded up her bath towel and, panting from her exertions, turned to us.

'That's got shot of him, and you won't be bothered again tonight. Next time he comes, do what I did. Flap something in his face. He doesn't like that. Nasty, dreamy creature, he is.'

'But . . .' Rodney was almost jumping up and down in bed with excitement, '. . . what . . . who is he?'

'A nasty old ghost, what did you imagine he was?' Mrs Fairweather's face expressed profound astonishment at our ignorance; 'one of them old monks that used to live here, donkey's years ago.'

'Gosh,' Rodney eyed the wall through which the monk had vanished, 'do you mean he'll come back?'

'More than likely.' The old lady had rejoined her husband in the doorway. 'But when he does, no waking me out of a deep sleep. Do as I say, flap something in his face, and above all, don't encourage him. Another thing,' she paused and waved an admonishing finger, 'there's no need to tell that Miss Fortesque about him. She looks as if she's frightened of her own shadow as it is. Now go to sleep, and no more nonsense.'

It was some time before we went to sleep.

'Harry,' Rodney repeated the question several times, 'what is a ghost?'

I made the same answer each time.

'I dunno.'

'It seems a good thing to be. I mean, being able to go through walls and dance in the air. I'd make Miss Fortesque jump out of her skin. I say, she must sleep like a log.'

'Her room is some distance away,' I pointed out.

'Still, all that racket I was making . . .' He yawned. 'Tomorrow, we'll ask her what a ghost is.'

'Mrs Fairweather said we were not to tell her about the ghost.'

'There's no need to tell her we've seen one, stupid. Just ask her what it is.'

Rodney tacked the question on to Henry the Eighth's wives next morning.

'Name Henry the Eighth's wives,' Miss Fortesque had instructed. Rodney had hastened to oblige.

'Catherine of Aragon, Anne Boleyn, Jane Seymour, Anne of Cleves, Catherine Howard, and Catherine Parr who survived him, but it was a near thing. Please, Miss Fortesque, what is a ghost?'

'Very good,' Miss Fortesque was nodding her approval, then suddenly froze. 'What!'

'What is a ghost?'

The frightened look crept back into her eyes, and I could see she suspected some horrible joke.

'Don't be silly, let's get on with the lesson.'

'But I want to know,' Rodney insisted, 'please, what is a ghost?'

'Well,' Miss Fortesque still was not happy, but clearly she considered it her duty to answer any intelligent question, 'it is said, a ghost is a spirit who is doomed to walk the earth after death.'

'Blimey!' Rodney scratched his head, 'a ghost is dead?'

'Of course – at least, so it is said. But it is all nonsense. Ghosts do not exist.'

'What!' Rodney's smile was wonderful to behold, 'you mean – you don't believe ghosts exist?'

'I know they don't,' Miss Fortesque was determined to leave the subject before it got out of hand. 'Ghosts are the result of ignorant superstition. Now, let us get on. Harry this time. How did Henry dispose of his wives?'

I stifled a yawn.

'Catherine of Aragon divorced, Anne Boleyn beheaded, Jane Seymour died, Anne of Cleves divorced, Catherine Howard beheaded, Catherine Parr . . .'

'I say, Harry,' Rodney remarked later that day, 'I bet Brownie was the odd man out.'

'Who?'

'Brownie, the monk. There's always one in big establishments. You remember at prep school last year, that chap Jenkins. He was lazy, stupid, never washed. The chances are, Brownie was the odd man out among the other monks. Probably never washed or shaved unless he was chivvied by the abbot, then when he died he hadn't the sense to realize there was some other place for him to go. So, he keeps hanging about here. Yes, I guess that's it. Brownie was the stupid one.'

'I don't think one should flap a towel in his face,' I said, 'it's not polite.'

'You don't have to be polite to a ghost,' Rodney scoffed, 'but I agree it's senseless. Next time he comes we'll find out more about him. I mean, he's not solid, is he? You saw how the towel went right through his head.'

It was several weeks before Brownie came again, and we

were a little worried that Mrs Fairweather had frightened him away for good. Then one night I was awakened by Rodney. He was standing by my bed, and as I awoke he lit the candle, his hand fair shaking with excitement.

'Is he back?' I asked, not yet daring to look for myself.

'Yep,' Rodney nodded, 'on the foot of your bed, as before. Come on, get up, we'll have some fun.'

I was not entirely convinced this was going to be fun, but I obediently clambered out of bed, then with some reluctance turned my head.

He was there, in exactly the same position as before, seated sideways on the bed, the cowl slipped back on to his shoulders, and staring at the left-hand wall.

'Why does he always sit in the same place?' I asked in a whisper.

'I expect this was the room he slept in, and more than likely his bed was in the same position as yours. I say, he does look weird. Let's have a closer look.'

Holding the candlestick well before him, Rodney went round the bed and peered into the monk's face. Rather fearfully, I followed him.

The face was podgy, deeply tanned, as though its owner had spent a lot of time out of doors, and the large brown eyes were dull and rather sad.

'I told you so,' Rodney said with a certain amount of satisfaction, 'he's stupid; spent most of his time day-dreaming while the other monks were chopping wood, getting in the harvest, or whatever things they got up to. I bet they bullied him, in a monkish sort of way.'

'I feel sorry for him,' I said, 'he looks so sad.'

'You would.' Rodney put the candle down. 'Let's

see what he's made of. Punch your hand into his ribs.'

I shook my head. 'Don't want to.'

'Go on, he won't hurt you. You're afraid.'

'I'm not.'

'Well, I'm going to have a go. Stand back, and let the dog see the rabbit.'

He rolled up his pyjama sleeve, took a deep breath, then gently brought his clenched fist into contact with the brown robe.

'Can't feel a thing,' he reported. 'Well, here goes.'

Fascinated, I saw his arm disappear into Brownie's stomach; first the fist, then the forearm, finally the elbow.

'Look round the back,' Rodney ordered, 'and see if my hand is sticking out of his spine.'

With a cautious look at Brownie's face, which so far had displayed no signs that he resented these liberties taken with his person, I peered round the brown-covered shoulders. Sure enough, there was Rodney's hand waving at me from the middle of the monk's back.

I nodded. 'I can see it.'

'Feels rather cold and damp,' Rodney said, and brought his arm out sideways. 'As I see it, nothing disturbs him unless something is flapped in his face. I expect the monks used to flap their robes at him, when they wanted to wake him up. Now you try.'

With some misgivings, I rolled up my sleeve and pushed my arm into Brownie's stomach, being careful to close my eyes first. There was an almost indefinable feeling of cold dampness, like putting my arm out of a window early on a spring morning. I heard Rodney laugh, and opened my eyes.

It is a very disturbing experience to say the least, to see your arm buried up to the elbow in a monk's stomach. I pulled it out quickly, determined to have nothing more to do with the entire business, but Rodney had only just begun.

'I'm going in head first,' he announced.

Before I had time to consider what he intended to do, he plunged his head through Brownie's left ribs, and in next to no time I saw his face grinning at me from the other side. It was really quite funny and, forgetting my former squeamishness, I begged to be allowed to have a go.

'All right,' Rodney agreed, 'but you start from the other side.'

We played happily at 'going through Brownie' for the next twenty minutes. Sideways, backwards, feet first, we went in all ways – the grand climax came when Rodney took up the same position as Brownie, and literally sat inside him. But there was one lesson we learnt: Brownie was undisturbed by our efforts, as long as his head was not touched. Once Rodney tried to reach up and sort of look through the phantom's eyes. At once the blank face took on an expression of intense alarm, the eyes moved, the mouth opened, and had not Rodney instantly withdrawn, I'm certain the ghost would have started his slow dance towards the left-hand wall.

But there is a limit to the amount of amusement one can derive from crawling through a ghost. After a while we sat down and took stock of the situation.

'I wonder if he would be disturbed if we jumped in him,' Rodney inquired wistfully.

I was against any such drastic contortion. 'Yes, it would be worse than flapping a towel in his face.'

'I suppose so,' Rodney relinquished the project with reluctance, then his face brightened. 'I say, let's show him to Miss Fortesque.'

'Oh no!' My heart went out to that poor, persecuted creature.

'Why not? In a way we would be doing her a service. After all, she doesn't believe in ghosts. It does people good to be proved they're wrong.'

'I dunno.'

'I'm going to her room,' Rodney got up, his eyes alive with mischievous excitement. 'I'll say there is someone in our room – no, that won't do – I'll say you've got tummy ache.'

'But that's a lie,' I objected.

'Well, you might have tummy ache, so it's only half a lie. You stay here, and don't frighten Brownie, in fact don't move.'

Thankfully, he left me the lighted candle, having thoughtfully provided himself with a torch, for there was no moon, and being alone in the dark with Brownie was still an alarming prospect. I sat down at the phantom's feet and peered up into that blank face. Yes, it was a stupid face, but can a person be blamed for being stupid? Apart from that, his eyes were very sad, or so they appeared to me, and I began to regret the silly tricks we had played on him. Minutes passed, then footsteps were ascending the stairs; Rodney's voice could be heard stressing the gravity of my mythical stomach ache, with Miss Fortesque occasionally interposing with a soft-spoken inquiry.

Rodney came in through the doorway, his face shining with excitement. Miss Fortesque followed, her expression one of deep concern. She stopped when she saw Brownie. Her face turned, if possible, a shade paler, and for a moment I thought she would faint.

'Who . . . ?' she began.

'Brownie,' Rodney announced. 'He's a ghost.'

'Don't talk such nonsense. Who is this man?'

'A ghost,' Rodney's voice rose. 'He is one of the monks who lived here ages ago. Look.'

He ran forward, stationed himself before the still figure and plunged his arm into its chest. Miss Fortesque gasped: 'Oh,' just once before she sank down on to the bed and closed her eyes. The grin died on Rodney's face, to be replaced by a look of alarmed concern.

'Please,' he begged, 'don't be frightened, he won't hurt you, honestly. Harry and I think he's lost. Too stupid to find his way to . . .' he paused, 'to wherever he ought to go.'

Miss Fortesque opened her eyes and took a deep breath. Though I was very young, I admired the way she conquered her fear, more, her abject terror, and rose unsteadily to her feet. She moved very slowly to where Brownie sat, then stared intently at the blank face.

'You have done a dreadful thing,' she said at last, 'to mock this poor creature. I am frightened, very frightened, but I must help him. Somehow, I must help him.'

'How?' inquired Rodney.

'I don't know.' She moved nearer and peered into the unblinking eyes. 'He looks like someone who is sleep-walking. How do you rouse him?'

'Touch his head. Mrs Fairweather flaps a towel in his face.'

Miss Fortesque raised one trembling hand and waved it gently before Brownie's face. He stirred uneasily, his eyes blinked, then, as the hand was waved again, flowed slowly upwards. Miss Fortesque gave a little cry and retreated a few steps.

'No.' She spoke in a voice only just above a whisper. 'Please, please listen.'

Brownie was already two feet above floor level, but he paused and looked back over one shoulder, while a look of almost comical astonishment appeared on his face.

'Please listen,' Miss Fortesque repeated, 'you can hear me, can't you?'

A leg drifted downwards, then he rotated so that he was facing the young woman, only he apparently forgot to descend to floor level. There was the faintest suggestion of a nod.

'You shouldn't be here,' Miss Fortesque continued. 'You, and . . . all your friends, died a long time ago. You ought to be . . . somewhere else.'

The expression was now one of bewilderment and Brownie looked helplessly round the room; his unspoken question was clear.

'Not in this house,' she shook her head, 'perhaps in heaven, I don't know, but certainly in the place where one goes to after death. Can't you try to find it?'

The shoulders came up into an expressive shrug, and Rodney snorted.

'I told you, he's too stupid.'

'Will you be quiet,' Miss Fortesque snapped, 'how can you be so cruel?' She turned to Brownie again. 'Forgive them, they are only children. Surely the other monks taught you about . . . Perhaps you did not understand. But you must leave this house. Go –' she gave a little cry of excitement, 'Go upwards! I'm sure that's right. Go up into the blue sky, away from this world; out among the stars, there you'll find the place. Now, I'm absolutely certain. Go out to the stars.'

Brownie was still poised in the air; his poor stupid face wore a perplexed frown as he pondered on Miss Fortesque's theory. Then, like the sun appearing from behind a cloud, a smile was born. A slow, rather jolly smile, accompanied by a nod, as though Brownie had at last remembered something important he had no business to have forgotten.

He straightened his legs, put both arms down flat with his hips, and drifted upwards, all the while smiling that jolly, idiotic grin, and nodding. His head disappeared into the ceiling, followed by his shoulders and then his hips. The last we saw were those two worn sandals. Miss Fortesque gave a loud gasp, then burst into tears. I did my best to comfort her.

'I'm sure you sent him in the right direction,' I said, 'he looked very pleased.'

'I bet he finishes up on the wrong star,' Rodney commented dourly. I turned on him.

'He won't, I just know he won't. He wasn't so dumb. Once Miss Fortesque sort of jolted his memory he was off like a shot.'

'Now, boys,' Miss Fortesque dried her eyes on her dressing-gown sleeve, 'to bed. Tomorrow we must pretend this never happened. In fact,' she shuddered, 'I'd like you to promise me you'll never mention the matter again – ever. Is that understood?'

We said, 'Yes,' and Rodney added, 'I think you're quite brave, honestly.'

She blushed, kissed us both quickly on our foreheads, then departed. Just before I drifted into sleep, I heard Rodney say:

'I wouldn't mind being a ghost. Imagine being able to drift up through the ceiling, and flying out to the stars. I can't wait to be dead.'

Miss Fortesque's theory must have been right. We never saw Brownie again.

Lost Hearts

M. R. James

It was, as far as I can ascertain, in September of the year 1811 that a post-chaise drew up before the door of Aswarby Hall, in the heart of Lincolnshire. The little boy who was the only passenger in the chaise, and who jumped out as soon as it had stopped, looked about him with the keenest curiosity during the short interval that elapsed between the ringing of the bell and the opening of the hall door. He saw a tall, square, red-brick house, built in the reign of Anne; a stone-pillared porch had been added in the purer classical style of 1790; the windows of the house were many, tall and narrow, with small panes and thick white woodwork. A pediment, pierced with a round window, crowned the front. There were wings to right and left, connected by curious glazed galleries, supported by colonnades, with the central block. These wings plainly contained the stables and offices of the house. Each was surmounted by an ornamental cupola with a gilded vane.

An evening light shone on the building, making the window-panes glow like so many fires. Away from the Hall in front stretched a flat park studded with oaks and fringed with firs, which stood out against the sky. The clock in the church-tower, buried in trees on the edge of the park, only its golden weather-cock catching the light, was striking six, and the sound came gently beating down the wind. It was altogether a pleasant impression, though tinged with the sort of melancholy appropriate to an evening in early autumn, that was conveyed to the mind of the boy who was standing in the porch waiting for the door to open to him.

The post-chaise had brought him from Warwickshire, where, some six months before, he had been left an orphan. Now, owing to the generous offer of his elderly cousin, Mr Abney, he had come to live at Aswarby. The offer was unexpected, because all who knew anything of Mr Abney looked upon him as a somewhat austere recluse, into whose steady-going household the advent of a small boy would import a new and, it seemed, incongruous element. The truth is that very little was known of Mr Abney's pursuits or temper. The Professor of Greek at Cambridge had been heard to say that no one knew more of the religious beliefs of the later pagans than did the owner of Aswarby. Certainly his library contained all the then available books bearing on the Mysteries, the Orphic poems, the worship of Mithras, and the Neo-Platonists. In the marble-paved hall stood a fine group of Mithras slaying a bull, which had been imported from the Levant at great expense by the owner. He had contributed a description of it to the *Gentleman's Magazine*, and he had written a remarkable series of articles in the *Critical Museum* on the superstitions of the Romans of the Lower Empire. He was looked upon, *in fine*, as a man wrapped up in his books, and it was a matter of great surprise among his neighbours that he could even have heard of his orphan cousin, Stephen Elliott, much more that he should have volunteered to make him an inmate of Aswarby Hall.

Whatever may have been expected by his neighbours, it is certain that Mr Abney – the tall, the thin, the austere – seemed inclined to give his young cousin a kindly reception. The moment the front door was opened he darted out of his study, rubbing his hands with delight.

'How are you, my boy? – how are you? How old are you?' said he – 'that is, you are not too much tired, I hope, by your journey to eat your supper?'

'No, thank you, sir,' said Master Elliott; 'I am pretty well.'

'That's a good lad,' said Mr Abney. 'And how old are you, my boy?'

It seemed a little odd that he should have asked the question twice in the first two minutes of their acquaintance.

'I'm twelve years old next birthday, sir,' said Stephen.

'And when is your birthday, my dear boy? Eleventh of September, eh? That's well – that's very well. Nearly a year hence, isn't it? I like – ha, ha! – I like to get these things down in my book. Sure it's twelve? Certain?'

'Yes, quite sure, sir.'

'Well, well! Take him to Mrs Bunch's room, Parkes, and let him have his tea – supper – whatever it is.'

'Yes, sir,' answered the staid Mr Parkes; and conducted Stephen to the lower regions.

Mrs Bunch was the most comfortable and human person whom Stephen had as yet met in Aswarby. She made him completely at home; they were great friends in a quarter of an hour: and great friends they remained. Mrs Bunch had been born in the neighbourhood some fifty-five years before the date of Stephen's arrival, and her residence at the Hall was of twenty years' standing. Consequently, if anyone knew the ins and outs of the house and the district, Mrs Bunch knew them; and she was by no means disinclined to communicate her information.

Certainly there were plenty of things about the Hall and the Hall gardens which Stephen, who was of an adventurous and inquiring turn, was anxious to have explained to him. 'Who built the temple at the end of the laurel walk? Who was the old man whose picture hung on the staircase, sitting at a table, with a skull under his hand?' These and many similar points were cleared up by the resources of Mrs Bunch's powerful intellect. There were others, however, of which the explanations furnished were less satisfactory.

One November evening Stephen was sitting by the fire in the housekeeper's room reflecting on his surroundings.

'Is Mr Abney a good man, and will he go to heaven?' he suddenly asked, with the peculiar confidence which children possess in the ability of their elders to settle these questions, the decision of which is believed to be reserved for other tribunals.

'Good? – bless the child!' said Mrs Bunch. 'Master's as kind a soul as ever I see! Didn't I never tell you of the little boy as he took in out of the street, as you may say, this seven years back? and the little girl, two years after I first come here?'

'No. Do tell me all about them, Mrs Bunch – now this minute!'

'Well,' said Mrs Bunch, 'the little girl I don't seem to recollect so much about. I know master brought her back with him from his walk one day, and give orders to Mrs Ellis, as was housekeeper then, as she should be took every care with. And the pore child hadn't no one belonging to her – she telled me so her own self – and here she lived with us a matter of three weeks it might be; and then, whether she were somethink of a gipsy in her blood or what not, but one morning she out of her bed afore any of us had opened an eye, and neither track nor yet trace of her have I set eyes on since. Master was wonderful put about, and had all the ponds dragged; but it's my belief she was had away by them gipsies, for there was singing round the house for as much as an hour the night she went, and Parkes, he declare as he heard them a-calling in the woods all that afternoon.

Dear, dear! a hodd child she was, so silent in her ways and all, but I was wonderful taken up with her, so domesticated she was – surprising.'

'And what about the little boy?' said Stephen.

'Ah, that pore boy!' sighed Mrs Bunch. 'He were a foreigner – Jevanny he called hisself – and he come a-tweaking his 'urdy-gurdy round and about the drive one winter day, and master 'ad him in that minute, and ast all about where he came from, and how old he was, and how he made his way, and where was his relatives, and all as kind as heart could wish. But it went the same way with him. They're a hunruly lot, them foreign nations, I do suppose, and he was off one fine morning just the same as the girl. Why he went and what he done was our question for as much as a year after; for he never took his 'urdy-gurdy, and there it lays on the shelf.'

The remainder of the evening was spent by Stephen in miscellaneous cross-examination of Mrs Bunch and in efforts to extract a tune from the hurdy-gurdy.

That night he had a curious dream. At the end of the passage at the top of the house, in which his bedroom was situated, there was an old disused bathroom. It was kept locked, but the upper half of the door was glazed, and, since the muslin curtains which used to hang there had long been gone, you could look in and see the lead-lined bath affixed to the wall on the right hand, with its head towards the window.

On the night of which I am speaking, Stephen Elliott found himself, as he thought, looking through the glazed door. The moon was shining through the window, and he was gazing at a figure which lay in the bath.

His description of what he saw reminds me of what I once

beheld myself in the famous vaults of St Michan's Church in Dublin, which possess the horrid property of preserving corpses from decay for centuries. A figure inexpressibly thin and pathetic, of a dusty leaden colour, enveloped in a shroud-like garment, the thin lips crooked into a faint and dreadful smile, the hands pressed tightly over the region of the heart.

As he looked upon it, a distant, almost inaudible moan seemed to issue from its lips, and the arms began to stir. The terror of the sight forced Stephen backwards, and he awoke to the fact that he was indeed standing on the cold boarded floor of the passage in the full light of the moon. With a courage which I do not think can be common among boys of his age, he went to the door of the bathroom to ascertain if the figure of his dream were really there. It was not, and he went back to bed.

Mrs Bunch was much impressed next morning by his story, and went so far as to replace the muslin curtain over the glazed door of the bathroom. Mr Abney, moreover, to whom he confided his experiences at breakfast, was greatly interested, and made notes of the matter in what he called 'his book'.

The spring equinox was approaching, as Mr Abney frequently reminded his cousin, adding that this had been always considered by the ancients to be a critical time for the young: that Stephen would do well to take care of himself, and to shut his bedroom window at night; and that Censorinus had some valuable remarks on the subject. Two incidents that occurred about this time made an impression upon Stephen's mind.

The first was after an unusually uneasy and oppressed

night that he had passed – though he could not recall any particular dream that he had had.

The following evening Mrs Bunch was occupying herself in mending his nightgown.

'Gracious me, Master Stephen!' she broke forth rather irritably, 'how do you manage to tear your nightdress all to flinders this way? Look here, sir, what trouble you do give to poor servants that have to darn and mend after you!'

There was indeed a most destructive and apparently wanton series of slits or scorings in the garment, which would undoubtedly require a skilful needle to make good. They were confined to the left side of the chest – long, parallel slits, about six inches in length, some of them not quite piercing the texture of the linen. Stephen could only express his entire ignorance of their origin: he was sure they were not there the night before.

'But,' he said, 'Mrs Bunch, they are just the same as the scratches on the outside of my bedroom door; and I'm sure I never had anything to do with making *them*.'

Mrs Bunch gazed at him open-mouthed, then snatched up a candle, departed hastily from the room, and was heard making her way upstairs. In a few minutes she came down.

'Well,' she said, 'Master Stephen, it's a funny thing to me how them marks and scratches can 'a' come there – too high up for any cat or dog to 'ave made 'em, much less a rat: for all the world like a Chinaman's finger-nails, as my uncle in the tea-trade used to tell us of when we was girls together. I wouldn't say nothing to master, not if I was you, Master Stephen, my dear; and just turn the key of the door when you go to your bed.'

'I always do, Mrs Bunch, as soon as I've said my prayers.'

'Ah, that's a good child: always say your prayers, and then no one can't hurt you.'

Herewith Mrs Bunch addressed herself to mending the injured nightgown, with intervals of meditation, until bed-time. This was on a Friday night in March 1812.

On the following evening the usual duet of Stephen and Mrs Bunch was augmented by the sudden arrival of Mr Parkes, the butler, who as a rule kept himself rather *to* himself in his own pantry. He did not see that Stephen was there: he was, moreover, flustered, and less slow of speech than was his wont.

'Master may get up his own wine, if he likes, of an evening,' was his first remark. 'Either I do it in the daytime or not at all, Mrs Bunch. I don't know what it may be: very like it's the rats, or the wind got into the cellars; but I'm not so young as I was, and I can't go through with it as I have done.'

'Well, Mr Parkes, you know it is a surprising place for the rats, is the Hall.'

'I'm not denying that, Mrs Bunch; and, to be sure, many a time I've heard the tale from the men in the shipyards about the rat that could speak. I never laid no confidence in that before; but tonight, if I'd demeaned myself to lay my ear to the door of the further bin, I could pretty much have heard what they was saying.'

'Oh, there, Mr Parkes, I've no patience with your fancies! Rats talking in the wine-cellar indeed!'

'Well, Mrs Bunch, I've no wish to argue with you: all I say is, if you choose to go to the far bin, and lay your ear to the door, you may prove my words this minute.'

'What nonsense you do talk, Mr Parkes – not fit for

children to listen to! Why, you'll be frightening Master Stephen there out of his wits.'

'What! Master Stephen?' said Parkes, awaking to the consciousness of the boy's presence. 'Master Stephen knows well enough when I'm a-playing a joke with you, Mrs Bunch.'

In fact, Master Stephen knew much too well to suppose that Parkes had in the first instance intended a joke. He was interested, not altogether pleasantly, in the situation; but all his questions were unsuccessful in inducing the butler to give any more detailed account of his experiences in the wine-cellar.

We have now arrived at 24 March 1812. It was a day of curious experiences for Stephen: a windy, noisy day, which filled the house and the gardens with a restless impression. As Stephen stood by the fence of the grounds, and looked out into the park, he felt as if an endless procession of unseen people were sweeping past him on the wind, borne on restlessly and aimlessly, vainly striving to stop themselves, to catch at something that might arrest their flight and bring them once again into contact with the living world of which they had formed a part. After luncheon that day Mr Abney said:

'Stephen, my boy, do you think you could manage to come to me tonight as late as eleven o'clock in my study? I shall be busy until that time, and I wish to show you something connected with your future life which it is most important that you should know. You are not to mention this matter to Mrs Bunch nor to anyone else in the house; and you had better go to your room at the usual time.'

Here was a new excitement added to life: Stephen eagerly grasped at the opportunity of sitting up till eleven o'clock. He looked in at the library door on his way upstairs that evening, and saw a brazier, which he had often noticed in the corner of the room, moved out before the fire; an old silver-gilt cup stood on the table, filled with red wine, and some written sheets of paper lay near it. Mr Abney was sprinkling some incense on the brazier from a round silver box as Stephen passed, but did not seem to notice his step.

The wind had fallen, and there was a still night and a full moon. At about ten o'clock Stephen was standing at the open window of his bedroom, looking out over the country. Still as the night was, the mysterious population of the distant moonlit woods was not yet lulled to rest. From time to time strange cries as of lost and despairing wanderers sounded from across the mere. They might be the notes of owls or water-birds, yet they did not quite resemble either sound. Were not they coming nearer? Now they sounded from the nearer side of the water, and in a few moments they seemed to be floating about among the shrubberies. Then they ceased; but just as Stephen was thinking of shutting the window and resuming his reading of *Robinson Crusoe*, he caught sight of two figures standing on the gravelled terrace that ran along the garden side of the Hall – the figures of a boy and girl, as it seemed; they stood side by side, looking up at the windows. Something in the form of the girl recalled irresistibly his dream of the figure in the bath. The boy inspired him with more acute fear.

Whilst the girl stood still, half smiling, with her hands clasped over her heart, the boy, a thin shape, with black hair

and ragged clothing, raised his arms in the air with an appearance of menace and of unappeasable hunger and longing. The moon shone upon his almost transparent hands, and Stephen saw that the nails were fearfully long and that the light shone through them. As he stood with his arms thus raised, he disclosed a terrifying spectacle. On the left side of his chest there opened a black and gaping rent; and there fell upon Stephen's brain, rather than upon his ear, the impression of one of those hungry and desolate cries that he had heard resounding over the woods of Aswarby all that evening. In another moment this dreadful pair had moved swiftly and noiselessly over the dry gravel, and he saw them no more.

Inexpressibly frightened as he was, he determined to take his candle and go down to Mr Abney's study, for the hour appointed for their meeting was near at hand. The study or library opened out of the front hall on one side, and Stephen, urged on by his terrors, did not take long in getting there. To effect an entrance was not so easy. The door was not locked, he felt sure, for the key was on the outside of it as usual. His repeated knocks produced no answer. Mr Abney was engaged: he was speaking. What! why did he try to cry out? and why was the cry choked in his throat? Had he, too, seen the mysterious children? But now everything was quiet, and the door yielded to Stephen's terrified and frantic pushing.

On the table in Mr Abney's study certain papers were found which explained the situation to Stephen Elliott when he was of an age to understand them. The most important sentences were as follows:

It was a belief very strongly and generally held by the ancients – of whose wisdom in these matters I have had such experience as induces me to place confidence in their assertions – that by enacting certain processes which to us moderns have something of a barbaric complexion, a very remarkable enlightenment of the spiritual faculties in man may be attained: that, for example, by absorbing the personalities of a certain number of his fellow-creatures, an individual may gain a complete ascendancy over those orders of spiritual beings which control the elemental forces of our universe.

It is recorded of Simon Magnus that he was able to fly in the air, to become invisible, or to assume any form he pleased, by the agency of the soul of a boy whom, to use the libellous phrase employed by the author of the *Clementine Recognitions*, he had 'murdered'. I find it set down, moreover, with considerable detail in the writings of Hermes Trismegistus, that similar happy results may be produced by the absorption of the hearts of not less than three human beings below the age of twenty-one years. To the testing of the truth of this receipt I have devoted the greater part of the last twenty years, selecting as the *corpora vilia* of my experiment such persons as could conveniently be removed without occasioning a sensible gap in society. The first step I effected by the removal of one Phoebe Stanley, a girl of gipsy extraction, on 24 March 1792. The second, by the removal of a wandering Italian lad, named Giovanni Paoli, on the night of 23 March 1805. The final 'victim' – to employ a word repugnant in the highest degree to my feelings – must be my cousin, Stephen Elliott. His day must be this 24 March 1812.

The best means of effecting the required absorption is to remove the heart from the *living* subject, to reduce it to ashes, and to mingle them with about a pint of some red wine, preferably port. The remains of the first two subjects, at least, it will be well to conceal: a disused bathroom or wine-cellar will be found convenient for such a purpose. Some annoyance may be experienced from the psychic portion of the subjects, which popular language dignifies with the name of ghosts. But the man of philosophic temperament – to whom alone the experiment is appropriate – will be little prone to attach importance to the feeble efforts of these beings to wreak their vengeance on him. I contemplate with the liveliest satisfaction the enlarged and emancipated existence which the experiment, if successful, will confer on me; not only placing me beyond the reach of human justice (so-called), but eliminating to a great extent the prospect of death itself.

Mr Abney was found in his chair, his head thrown back, his face stamped with an expression of rage, fright, and mortal pain. In his left side was a terrible lacerated wound, exposing the heart. There was no blood on his hands, and a long knife that lay on the table was perfectly clean. A savage wild-cat might have inflicted the injuries. The window of the study was open, and it was the opinion of the coroner that Mr Abney had met his death by the agency of some wild creature. But Stephen Elliott's study of the papers I have quoted led him to a very different conclusion.

Tea at Ravensburgh

Joan Aiken

'Bother,' said Mrs Armitage, reading her mid-morning mail. She took the letter that had annoyed her and went upstairs. Through a closed door came the sound of a typewriter. She tapped on the door and went in. Immediately the typing ceased.

The room she had entered was large and sunny, with a huge dormer window taking up most of one side. It was empty, save for a typing table, a portable typewriter and chair, and some shelves of books.

'Oh, Mr Peake,' said Mrs Armitage, 'I'm terribly sorry to disturb you at this hour of the morning, but would you mind if I used the typewriter for five minutes? I must just write a note to Harriet.'

There was an offended silence.

'It's *most* wicked of me, and I won't do it again,' Mrs Armitage went on placatingly, 'but my wretched old Aunt Adelaide has just cabled from the south of France asking me to meet her in London on Saturday, so I shan't be able to go down and take Harriet out from school this week-end. She'll be cross, I'm afraid. Are you sitting in the chair?'

'No, I'm not,' said a voice behind her shoulder. Mrs Armitage jumped. Although she had known him for twenty years she was never quite used to not knowing where Mr Peake was.

'It's most tiresome,' she said, rattling away at the keys, 'I'd much rather see Harriet, but Aunt Adelaide is so very rich that it would be foolish to offend her.'

'Nevertheless it seems hard that the little wench should lose her holiday,' said Mr Peake. ''Tis a good child. Last holidays she mended the toes of my carpet slippers until I could not tell where the holes had been.' He stuck out his invisible feet and regarded them with satisfaction.

'Well I know,' agreed Harriet's mother, 'but my husband can't go, he has a meeting of the Grass Growers' Association, and Mark is in quarantine for whooping cough.'

'I shall escort her out,' announced Mr Peake.

Mrs Armitage looked startled.

'Well – that's very sweet of you,' she answered dubiously. 'But are you sure you'll be able to manage?'

'Madame, you forget that I was once an explorer and sailed to the New World. What terrors would a female boarding establishment have for me?'

'In that case I'll add a P.S. and say that you are coming instead. Harriet *will* be excited. And you can take her a spare pair of socks and a pot of gooseberry jam. There.' She flipped her letter out of the machine, quickly addressed an envelope to Miss Armitage, Silverside School, Ham Street, Dorset, and stood up.

'Now perhaps,' said Mr Peake as she left the room, 'I can get on with my memoirs.' But he said it to himself, for he was a polite man.

Mr Peake was the Armitages' lodger, and if he has not been mentioned before, it is because he was so very quiet and unobtrusive that the family hardly noticed his existence. He had one room, with use of Mrs Armitage's typewriter in the mornings, and he hardly ever came downstairs. He had lived in the house for three hundred years, ever since his death in fact, and was thought to be writing his autobiography, though as it was invisible no one had read it. He had been a sailor and explorer and a friend of Drake, so there was plenty to write about.

When the Armitage family first moved into the house they took over Mr Peake from the previous owners. Harriet was a baby at the time, and the nursemaid had left in hysterics that week because one night when Harriet was teething she had come up to the nursery and seen Mr Peake walking to and fro hushing Harriet in his arms; or at least she had seen Harriet, for of course no one saw Mr Peake.

He had always remained very fond of Harriet ever since and used to give her odd little presents which he called fairings or baubles. When she had measles he sat by her bed reading to her for hours and hours. No one had ever known Mr Peake go to sleep.

Harriet was devoted to Mr Peake, but just the same, she was a little doubtful at the thought of being taken out from school by him. She had not been at Silverside very long, and did not want to get a reputation for peculiarity. It was very disappointing that her mother was obliged to go and meet Aunt Adelaide, as Mrs Armitage always made a good impression – she arrived punctually, wore the right sort of hat, made the right sort of remarks (and not too many of them) when she was taken round the school, and had tea with Harriet in the right places. It was hoped that Mr Peake would behave in an equally exemplary manner, but Harriet was afraid that he might seem eccentric to the rest of the school.

On the following Saturday she hung about in the front hall, hoping to catch him when he arrived. She did not want the difficulty of explaining about an invisible bell-ringer to one of the housemaids. Unfortunately members of the junior classes were not supposed to loiter in the hallway

and she had to keep pretending to be looking to see if there were any letters for her on the hall table, and then walk briskly up the front stairs and run hurriedly down the back stairs. After one of these descents she was lucky enough to see a pot of gooseberries and a pair of her mother's knitted socks approaching up the front steps, and was just in time to intercept Mr Peake before he rang the bell.

'It *is* nice to see you,' she said (no one ever remembered to adapt their speech to Mr Peake's peculiarity). 'Let me take that jam from you and then I have to report that I am going out to my house-mistress and we can be off.'

'I should admire to see a little of this female academy of learning, if it is convenient,' said the visitor. 'Such things have come in since my day.'

'Oh blow,' thought Harriet. Luckily on a Saturday afternoon she could rely on the place being fairly well deserted but two tiny juniors squeaked as she showed him round the gymnasium:

'Coo, listen to Harriet Armitage talking to herself. She must be going crackers!'

Harriet swept Mr Peake off to the library before he had half finished gazing at the ropes and the parallel bars.

Talking in the library was normally forbidden but a certain amount of latitude was allowed when visitors were being shown round. Mr Peake took great interest in the historical section and asked dozens of questions. Harriet noticed with alarm that Madeline Bogg, the Head Girl, who was working for a history examination, was in the next alcove and looking angrily in their direction.

'Harriet, will you stop making all that noise, please. I shall have to give you a hundred lines for talking in here.'

'But I have a visitor with me.'

'Don't talk nonsense, please.'

'Here, give her these lines,' said Mr Peake's voice in her ear. 'Doubtless the subject-matter is of no importance? I always travel with some reading material.' And he pulled out a parchment (from his doublet presumably), and passed it to Harriet, who handed it on to Madeline, absently noticing that it seemed to be about ship money. Madeline's jaw dropped.

'Where in the name of goodness did you get this,' she began. 'It's just the subject I was reading up –' but Harriet quickly dragged Mr Peake away and persuaded him that there was nothing else in the school worth looking at. She reported herself to her house-mistress and they went out into the little town of Ham Street where Harriet was quickly pounced on by two senior girls coming back from shopping.

'Harriet! What are you doing out by yourself? You know it's not allowed.'

'I'm not by myself, I'm with Mr Peake,' Harriet said miserably.

'Be at ease, the little wench is under my care,' Mr Peake reassured them.

'Mr Peake's had a rather bad cold – that's why you can't see him very well,' Harriet said desperately.

'I can't see him at all,' said Gertrude, the elder girl.

'Perhaps this will certify you of my presence, my fair sceptic.' Mr Peake presented her with a flower, apparently from his buttonhole. It was something like a wild rose but white, with a very sweet scent. They left Gertrude and her friend staring at it in perplexity and walked on.

Harriet decided that it would be best if they went to the cinema. It was something of a strain being out with Mr Peake, and she felt that sitting down in the sheltering dark would be a relief. She suggested this plan to him.

'I have never been to one of these places,' he replied, 'but one is never too old to do something new. Let us go by all means.'

When they came to the Paramount, Ham Street's only

cinema, they found that it was showing *The Nineteenth Man*, an 'A' film.

'Two two-and-three's, please,' said Mr Peake, prompted by Harriet.

'You can't go in without an adult, ducks,' said the cashier, looking through him at Harriet. 'Sorry, it's a smasher, but the manager's just over there.'

'But I've got an adult here – he's in front of me,' explained Harriet rather hopelessly. Mr Peake rapped with his two half-crowns on the cash desk and the cashier let out a shriek which fetched over the manager.

'Two seats in the pit, if you please,' demanded Mr Peake.

'Now, now, none of your nasty ventriloquism tricks here,' he said, scowling at Harriet. 'Go on – hop it, afore I rings your headmistress.'

'This town boasts a river, does it not?' inquired Mr Peake, as they walked along the High Street. 'Should we adventure in a boat?'

Harriet privately thought it rather a chilly pursuit for a November afternoon, but perhaps Mr Peake was pining for a taste of his nautical past. She tucked her arm through his, feeling rather sorry for him, and they went down to the boat-house by the bridge where a few punts and canoes were being hired out.

'No one under the age of sixteen to go out unaccompanied by an adult,' said the man pointing inflexibly to a framed copy of the By-Laws on a notice board.

'But I *am* accompanied by an adult.'

'One who, moreover, has countless times weathered the Spanish Main,' added Mr Peake. 'Be more polite to your betters, sirrah.'

NOTICE
BY-LAWS

'Blimey,' said the man, scratching his head. 'Ought to go on the halls, you ought. Run along, now scram, before I give you in charge.'

'It is an uncourteous city,' said Mr Peake, as they stood irresolutely on the bridge.

'*I* know,' exclaimed Harriet, seeing a bus approaching. 'We'll go and look at Ravensburgh Castle – I've always wanted to.'

They had no trouble on the bus, apart from the conductor's displeasure with the Queen Anne sixpence which Mr Peake absently tendered him (change from rent paid to the last landlord but five, he explained to Harriet). Presently, as the bus filled up, people began to look meaningly at the empty seat next to Harriet, but Mr Peake solved this problem by taking her on his lap. It is a very strange feeling to ride on a ghost's lap in a bus.

Once Mr Peake remarked: 'The horseless carriages in this country are indifferent well sprung,' and the woman on the seat in front of them jumped and looked round at Harriet indignantly.

The sky was clouding when they reached Ravensburgh on its hill, and it was almost cold enough for snow. Harriet shivered and wished that they were allowed to wear duffle coats instead of uniform ones.

'Shall we go up on the ramparts?' Mr Peake inquired. 'I believe one could achieve a view of the sea from there.'

As they were making the circuit of the top they heard shouts from below, and gathered that the uniformed attendant was trying to tell Harriet that she should not be up there on her own.

'I fear this is not a happy outing for you,' said poor Mr Peake.

'Oh no, I'm loving it,' lied Harriet gallantly. As a matter of fact she did feel that to walk in the icy dusk, hand in hand with a spectre round the battlements of Ravensburgh was rather a grand thing to do, even though the spectre was such an old friend as Mr Peake. But she would have liked her tea, and wondered what sort of reception they would have if they went into a cafe.

They came down to a wide room which had once been an upstairs banqueting hall.

'Why, bless my soul,' said Mr Peake, pausing. 'If that isn't – or is it – yes it is – my old boon companion, Sir Giles Harkness!'

'Where?' asked Harriet, looking all round and seeing nothing.

But Mr Peake had left her side and was exclaiming:

'Giles, my old messmate. How fares it with you?'

'Gregory! Gregory Peake, by my halidome! Well met after three hundred years. What brings you here? You must come and meet my lady – we lodge in the East Tower here. Do you remember that time off Madeira when we were in the pinnace and we saw three galleons coming up to windward?'

They launched out into a flood of reminiscence.

Oh, dear, thought Harriet, bored and shivering. Now they'll go on for hours; grown-ups always do.

She tried to climb into one of the embrasures, slipped, stumbled, and turned her ankle rather severely.

'What ails you, lass?' said Mr Peake, turning from his conversation. 'Oh, Giles, this is my little godchild, Mistress Harriet Armitage.'

'Your servant, Madame,' said the invisible Sir Giles, gravely. 'But there is something amiss? You have injured your foot? My lady shall bind it up straightway.'

Between them the two friends supported Harriet back to the rooms in the East Tower, never for one moment ceasing their flow of chat.

'And do you remember when Francis boarded you in the night and stole all your powder and ball and was away before dawn with none of your men any the wiser? Ah, Frank was a rare one for a jest.'

In the East Tower a lady with a very friendly voice skilfully bound up Harriet's ankle with what felt like a strip of silk.

It was curious to sit among people that one could not see and listen to them talking. Harriet did not think that she would like it for long. She felt inquisitively at the heavy carved arms of her chair, which she could not see either, and wondered if they were made of pale bright new oak.

'Ah, here is our little Hubert,' said Lady Harkness. 'He and the little maid should fadge well together – th'are much of an age.'

As usual on such occasions Harriet took an instantaneous unreasoning dislike to little Hubert. She was sure that he was a pale, puffy little boy in a ruff, and imagined him staring at her with his finger in his mouth.

Comfits were served round, very sweet and chewy, and drinks of hippocras, which Harriet did not care for. Hubert snatched a bit of Harriet's comfit while his mother was busy pouring out drinks, and Harriet dealt him what she hoped was a kick on the shin – she heard him squeak.

Then his elder brother Giles came in, a cheerful-sounding

boy who told Harriet about his boat, which he kept on the estuary, and invited her to go sailing with him next summer.

'I will if I can,' she promised, wondering if one can go sailing with a ghost. The whole party was becoming more and more dreamlike.

'Mr Peake,' she said, 'I'm afraid we should be going, as I haven't got permission to be out late.' She stood up, and then let out a cry as her ankle gave way under her.

'The wench can't walk on that ankle,' said Sir Giles. 'I'll lend you my mare, Black Peg – she'll have you home like a flash of lightning and find her own way back here again.'

'We are greatly obliged to you,' replied Mr Peake.

They left amid cordial invitations to come again.

As far as Harriet could make out, Black Peg had wings; they could not of course be seen, but she could feel feathers. She wondered if the mare was any relation of Pegasus.

They covered the distance to Ham Street in ten minutes, though it had taken an hour to come by bus. It was a pity that Black Peg sailed through the dining-room window. To be deposited by a ghost horse and rider in the middle of a school Saturday-night supper is not the best way to avoid a reputation for peculiarity.

'Harriet,' said the house-mistress coldly. 'Your godfather did not go to see the headmistress, as you should have told him to do before he took you out. And please get rid of that invisible horse and eat your supper.'

Black Peg galloped off through the window again, thinking of spectral oats in her phantom stable no doubt, and Harriet sat down miserably to cold spam and beetroot.

It was all right, though. Miss Drogly pronounced Mr

Peake to be a most interesting and delightful man – history was her own subject, and they had a long chat about the Duke of Medina Sidonia. And Mr Peake gave Harriet a dear little pouncet box with a clove orange in it before leaving, and she hugged him and said it had been a lovely party and promised to starch all his ruffs for him next holidays.

Next week Harriet had a letter from her mother.

'Aunt Adelaide was sorry that she had unintentionally prevented our outing, and asked me to send you this to make amends.'

This was sent under separate cover and turned out to be a small folding helicopter, so Harriet's reputation for being a perfectly ordinary girl with normal healthy interests was quite restored.

School for the Unspeakable

Manly Wade Wellman

Bart Setwick dropped off the train at Carrington and stood for a moment on the station platform, an honest-faced, well-knit lad in tweeds. This little town and its famous school would be his home for the next eight months; but which way to the school? The sun had set, and he could barely see the shop signs across Carrington's modest main street. He hesitated, and a soft voice spoke at his very elbow:

'Are you for the school?'

Startled, Bart Setwick wheeled. In the grey twilight stood another youth, smiling thinly and waiting as if for an answer. The stranger was all of nineteen years old – that meant maturity to young Setwick, who was fifteen – and his pale face had shrewd lines to it. His tall, shambling body was clad in high-necked jersey and unfashionably tight trousers. Bart Setwick skimmed him with the quick, appraising eye of young America.

'I just got here,' he replied. 'My name's Setwick.'

'Mine's Hoag.' Out came a slender hand. Setwick took it and found it froggy-cold, with a suggestion of steel-wire muscles. 'Glad to meet you. I came down on the chance someone would drop off the train. Let me give you a lift to the school.'

Hoag turned away, felinely light for all his ungainliness, and led his new acquaintance around the corner of the little wooden railway station. Behind the structure, half hidden in its shadow, stood a shabby buggy with a lean bay horse in the shafts.

'Get in,' invited Hoag, but Bart Setwick paused for a moment. His generation was not used to such vehicles. Hoag chuckled and said, 'Oh, this is only a school wrinkle. We run to funny customs. Get in.'

Setwick obeyed. 'How about my trunk?'

'Leave it.' The taller youth swung himself in beside Setwick and took the reins. 'You'll not need it tonight.'

He snapped his tongue and the bay horse stirred, drew them around and off down a bush-lined road. Its hoofbeats were oddly muffled.

They turned a corner, another, and came into open country. The lights of Carrington, newly kindled against the night, hung behind like a constellation settled down to Earth. Setwick felt a hint of chill that did not seem to fit the September evening.

'How far is the school from town?' he asked.

'Four or five miles,' Hoag replied in his hushed voice. 'That was deliberate on the part of the founders – they wanted to make it hard for the students to get to town for larks. It forced us to dig up our own amusements.' The pale face creased in a faint smile, as if this were a pleasantry. 'There's just a few of the right sort on hand tonight. By the way, what did you get sent out for?'

Setwick frowned his mystification. 'Why, to go to school. Dad sent me.'

'But what for? Don't you know that this is a high-class prison prep? Half of us are lunkheads that need poking along, the other half are fellows who got in scandals somewhere else. Like me.' Again Hoag smiled.

Setwick began to dislike his companion. They rolled a mile or so in silence before Hoag again asked a question:

'Do you go to church, Setwick?'

The new boy was afraid to appear priggish, and made a careless show with, 'Not very often.'

'Can you recite anything from the Bible,' Hoag's soft voice took on an anxious tinge.

'Not that I know of.'

'Good,' was the almost hearty response. 'As I was saying,

there's only a few of us at the school tonight – only three, to be exact. And we don't like Bible-quoters.'

Setwick laughed, trying to appear sage and cynical. 'Isn't Satan reputed to quote the Bible to his own—'

'What do you know about Satan?' interrupted Hoag. He turned full on Setwick, studying him with intent, dark eyes. Then, as if answering his own question: 'Little enough, I'll bet. Would you like to know about him?'

'Sure I would,' replied Setwick, wondering what the joke would be.

'I'll teach you after a while,' Hoag promised cryptically, and silence fell again.

Half a moon was well up as they came in sight of a dark jumble of buildings.

'Here we are,' announced Hoag, and then, throwing back his head, he emitted a wild, wordless howl that made Setwick almost jump out of the buggy. 'That's to let the others know we're coming,' he explained. 'Listen!'

Back came a seeming echo of the howl, shrill, faint and eerie. The horse wavered in its muffled trot, and Hoag clucked it back into step. They turned in at a driveway well grown up in weeds, and two minutes more brought them up to the rear of the closest building. It was dim grey in the wash of moonbeams, with blank inky rectangles for windows. Nowhere was there a light, but as the buggy came to a halt Setwick saw a young head pop out of a window on the lower floor.

'Here already, Hoag?' came a high, reedy voice.

'Yes,' answered the youth at the reins, 'and I've brought a new man with me.'

Thrilling a bit to hear himself called a man, Setwick alighted.

'His name's Setwick,' went on Hoag. 'Meet Andoff, Setwick. A great friend of mine.'

Andoff flourished a hand in greeting and scrambled out over the window-sill. He was chubby and squat and even paler than Hoag, with a low forehead beneath lank, wet-looking hair, and black eyes set wide apart in a fat, stupid-looking face. His shabby jacket was too tight for him, and beneath worn knickers his legs and feet were bare. He might have been an overgrown thirteen or an undeveloped eighteen.

'Felcher ought to be along in half a second,' he volunteered.

'Entertain Setwick while I put up the buggy,' Hoag directed him.

Andoff nodded, and Hoag gathered the lines in his hands, but paused for a final word.

'No funny business yet, Andoff,' he cautioned seriously.

'Setwick, don't let this lard-bladder rag you or tell you wild stories until I come back.'

Andoff laughed shrilly. 'No, no wild stories,' he promised. 'You'll do the talking, Hoag.'

The buggy trundled away, and Andoff swung his fat, grinning face to the new arrival.

'Here comes Felcher,' he announced. 'Felcher, meet Setwick.'

Another boy had bobbed up, it seemed, from nowhere. Setwick had not seen him come around the corner of the building, or slip out of a door or window. He was probably as old as Hoag, or older, but so small as to be almost a dwarf, and frail to boot. His most notable characteristic was his hairiness. A great mop covered his head, brushed over his neck and ears, and hung unkemptly to his bright, deepset eyes. His lips and cheeks were spread with a rank down, and a curly thatch peeped through the unbuttoned collar of his soiled white shirt. The hand he offered Setwick was almost simian in its shagginess and in the hardness of its palm. Too, it was cold and damp. Setwick remembered the same thing of Hoag's handclasp.

'We're the only ones here so far,' Felcher remarked. His voice, surprisingly deep and strong for so small a creature, rang like a great bell.

'Isn't even the headmaster here?' inquired Setwick, and at that the other two began to laugh uproariously, Andoff's fife-squeal rendering an obligato to Felcher's bell-boom. Hoag, returning, asked what the fun was.

'Setwick asks,' groaned Felcher, 'why the headmaster isn't here to welcome him.'

More fife-laughter and bell-laughter.

'I doubt if Setwick would think the answer was funny,' Hoag commented, and then chuckled softly himself.

Setwick, who had been well brought up, began to grow nettled.

'Tell me about it,' he urged, in what he hoped was a bleak tone, 'and I'll join your chorus of mirth.'

Felcher and Andoff gazed at him with eyes strangely eager and yearning. Then they faced Hoag.

'Let's tell him,' they both said at once, but Hoag shook his head.

'Not yet. One thing at a time. Let's have the song first.'

They began to sing. The first verse of their offering was

obscene, with no pretence of humour to redeem it. Setwick had never been squeamish, but he found himself definitely repelled. The second verse seemed less objectionable, but it hardly made sense:

'All they tried to teach here
Now goes untaught.
Ready, steady, each here,
Knowledge we sought.
What they called disaster
Killed us not, O master!
Rule us, we beseech here,
Eye, hand and thought.'

It was something like a hymn, Setwick decided, but before what altar would such hymns be sung? Hoag must have read that question in his mind.

'You mentioned Satan in the buggy on the way out,' he recalled, his knowing face hanging like a mask in the half-dimness close to Setwick. 'Well, that was a Satanist song.'

'It was? Who made it?'

'I did,' Hoag informed him. 'How do you like it?'

Setwick made no answer. He tried to sense mockery in Hoag's voice, but could not find it. 'What,' he asked finally, 'does all this Satanist singing have to do with the head-master?'

'A lot,' came back Felcher deeply, and 'A lot,' squealed Andoff.

Hoag gazed from one of his friends to the others, and for the first time he smiled broadly. It gave him a toothy look.

'I believe,' he ventured quietly but weightily, 'that we might as well let Setwick in on the secret of our little circle.'

Here it would begin, the new boy decided – the school

hazing of which he had heard and read so much. He had anticipated such things with something of excitement, even eagerness, but now he wanted none of them. He did not like his three companions, and he did not like the way they approached whatever it was they intended to do. He moved backward a pace or two, as if to retreat.

Swift as darting birds, Hoag and Andoff closed in at either elbow. Their chill hands clutched him and suddenly he felt light-headed and sick. Things that had been clear in the moonlight went hazy and distorted.

'Come on and sit down, Setwick,' invited Hoag, as though from a great distance. His voice did not grow loud or harsh, but it embodied real menace. 'Sit on that window-sill. Or would you like us to carry you?'

At the moment Setwick wanted only to be free of their touch, and so he walked unresistingly to the sill and scrambled up on it. Behind him was the blackness of an unknown chamber, and at his knees gathered the three who seemed so eager to tell him their private joke.

'The headmaster was a proper churchgoer,' began Hoag, as though he were the spokesman for the group. 'He didn't have any use for devils or devil-worship. Went on record against them when he addressed us in chapel. That was what started us.'

'Right,' nodded Andoff, turning up his fat, larval face. 'Anything he outlawed, we wanted to do. Isn't that logic?'

'Logic and reason,' wound up Felcher. His hairy right hand twiddled on the sill near Setwick's thigh. In the moonlight it looked like a big, nervous spider.

Hoag resumed. 'I don't know of any prohibition of his it was easier or more fun to break.'

Setwick found that his mouth had gone dry. His tongue could barely moisten his lips. 'You mean,' he said, 'that you began to worship devils?'

Hoag nodded happily, like a teacher at an apt pupil. 'One vacation I got a book on the cult. The three of us studied it, then began ceremonies. We learned the charms and spells, forward and backward –'

'They're twice as good backward,' put in Felcher, and Andoff giggled.

'Have you any idea, Setwick,' Hoag almost cooed, 'what it was that appeared in our study the first time we burned wine and sulphur, with the proper words spoken over them?'

Setwick did not want to know. He clenched his teeth. 'If you're trying to scare me,' he managed to growl out, 'it certainly isn't going to work.'

All three laughed once more, and began to chatter out their protestations of good faith.

'I swear that we're telling the truth, Setwick,' Hoag assured him. 'Do you want to hear it, or don't you?'

Setwick had very little choice in the matter, and he realized it. 'Oh, go ahead,' he capitulated, wondering how it would do to crawl backward from the sill into the darkness of the room.

Hoag, leaned toward him, with the air as of one confiding. 'The headmaster caught us. Caught us red-handed.'

'Book open, fire burning,' chanted Felcher.

'He had something very fine to say about the vengeance of heaven,' Hoag went on. 'We got to laughing at him. He worked up a frenzy. Finally he tried to take heaven's vengeance into his own hands – tried to visit it on us, in a very primitive way. But it didn't work.'

Andoff was laughing immoderately, his fat arms across his bent belly.

'He thought it worked,' he supplemented between high gurgles, 'but it didn't.'

'Nobody could kill us,' Felcher added. 'Not after the oaths we'd taken, and the promises that had been made us.'

'What promises?' demanded Setwick, who was struggling hard not to believe. 'Who made you any promises?'

'Those we worshipped,' Felcher told him. If he was simulating earnestness, it was a supreme bit of acting. Setwick, realizing this, was more daunted than he cared to show.

'When did all these things happen?' was his next question.

'When?' echoed Hoag. 'Oh, years and years ago.'

'Years and years ago,' repeated Andoff.

'Long before you were born,' Felcher assured him.

They were standing close together, their backs to the moon that shone in Setwick's face. He could not see their expressions clearly. But their three voices – Hoag's soft, Felcher's deep and vibrant, Andoff's high and squeaky – were absolutely serious.

'I know what you're arguing within yourself,' Hoag announced somewhat smugly. 'How can we, who talk about those many past years, seem so young? That calls for an explanation, I'll admit.' He paused, as if choosing words. 'Time – for us – stands still. It came to a halt on that very night, Setwick; the night our headmaster tried to put an end to our worship.'

'And to us,' smirked the gross-bodied Andoff, with his usual air of self-congratulation at capping one of Hoag's statements.

'The worship goes on,' pronounced Felcher, in the same chanting manner that he had affected once before. 'The worship goes on, and we go on, too.'

'Which brings us to the point,' Hoag came in briskly. 'Do you want to throw in with us, Setwick? – make the fourth of this lively little party?'

'No, I don't,' snapped Setwick vehemently.

They fell silent, and gave back a little – a trio of bizarre silhouettes against the pale moonglow. Setwick could see the flash of their staring eyes among the shadows of their faces. He knew that he was afraid, but hid his fear. Pluckily he dropped from the sill to the ground. Dew from the grass spattered his sock-clad ankles between oxfords and trouser-cuffs.

'I guess it's my turn to talk,' he told them levelly. 'I'll make it short. I don't like you, nor anything you've said. And I'm getting out of here.'

'We won't let you,' said Hoag, hushed but emphatic.

'We won't let you,' murmured Andoff and Felcher together, as though they had rehearsed it a thousand times.

Setwick clenched his fists. His father had taught him to box. He took a quick, smooth stride toward Hoag and hit him hard in the face. Next moment all three had flung themselves upon him. They did not seem to strike or grapple or tug, but he went down under their assault. The shoulders of his tweed coat wallowed in sand, and he smelled crushed weeds. Hoag, on top of him, pinioned his arms with a knee on each bicep. Felcher and Andoff were stooping close.

Glaring up in helpless rage, Setwick knew once and for all that this was no schoolboy prank. Never did practical jokers gather around their victim with such staring, green-gleaming eyes, such drawn jowls, such quivering lips.

Hoag bared white fangs. His pointed tongue quested once over them.

'Knife!' he muttered, and Felcher fumbled in a pocket, then passed him something that sparkled in the moonlight.

Hoag's lean hand reached for it, then whipped back. Hoag had lifted his eyes to something beyond the huddle. He choked and whimpered inarticulately, sprang up from Setwick's labouring chest, and fell back in awkward haste. The others followed his shocked stare, then as suddenly cowered and retreated in turn.

'It's the master!' wailed Andoff.

'Yes,' roared a gruff new voice. 'Your old headmaster – and I've come back to master *you*!'

Rising upon one elbow, the prostrate Setwick saw what they had seen – a tall, thick-bodied figure in a long dark coat, topped with a square, distorted face and a tousle of white locks. Its eyes glittered with their own pale, hard light. As it advanced slowly and heavily it emitted a snigger of murderous joy. Even at first glance Setwick was aware that it cast no shadow.

'I am in time,' mouthed the newcomer. 'You were going to kill this poor boy.'

Hoag had recovered and made a stand. 'Kill him?' he quavered, seeming to fawn before the threatening presence. 'No. We'd have given him life –'

'You call it life!' trumpeted the long-coated one. 'You'd have sucked out his blood to teem your own dead veins, damned him to your filthy condition. But I'm here to prevent you!'

A finger pointed, huge and knuckly, and then came a

torrent of language. To the nerve-stunned Setwick it sounded like a bit from the New Testament, or perhaps from the Book of Common Prayer. All at once he remembered Hoag's avowed dislike for such quotations.

His three erstwhile assailants reeled as if before a high wind that chilled or scorched. 'No, no! Don't!' they begged wretchedly.

The square old face gaped open and spewed merciless laughter. The knuckly finger traced a cross in the air, and the trio wailed in chorus as though the sign had been drawn upon their flesh with a tongue of flame.

Hoag dropped to his knees. 'Don't!' he sobbed.

'I have power,' mocked their tormentor. 'During years shut up I won it, and now I'll use it.' Again a triumphant burst of mirth. 'I know you're damned and can't be killed, but you can be tortured! I'll make you crawl like worms before I'm done with you!'

Setwick gained his shaky feet. The long coat and the blocky head leaned toward him.

'Run, you!' dinned a rough roar in his ears. 'Get out of here - and thank God for the chance!'

Setwick ran, staggering. He blundered through the weeds of the driveway, gained the road beyond. In the distance gleamed the lights of Carrington. As he turned his face toward them and quickened his pace he began to weep, chokingly, hysterically, exhaustingly.

He did not stop running until he reached the platform in front of the station. A clock across the street struck ten, in a deep voice not unlike Felcher's. Setwick breathed deeply, fished out his handkerchief and mopped his face. His hand was quivering like a grass stalk in a breeze.

'Beg pardon!' came a cheery hail. 'You must be Setwick.'

As once before on this same platform, he whirled around with startled speed. Within touch of him stood a broad-shouldered man of thirty or so, with horn-rimmed spectacles. He wore a neat Norfolk jacket and flannels. A short briar pipe was clamped in a good-humoured mouth.

'I'm Collins, one of the masters at the school,' he introduced himself. 'If you're Setwick, you've had us worried. We expected you on that seven o'clock train, you know. I dropped down to see if I couldn't trace you.'

Setwick found a little of his lost wind. 'But I've – been to the school,' he mumbled protestingly. His hand, still trembling, gestured vaguely along the way he had come.

Collins threw back his head and laughed, then apologized. 'Sorry,' he said. 'It's no joke if you really had all that walk for nothing. Why, that old place is deserted – used to be a catch-all for incorrigible rich boys. They closed it about fifty years ago, when the headmaster went mad and killed three of his pupils. As a matter of coincidence, the master himself died just this afternoon, in the state hospital for the insane.'

The Emissary

Ray Bradbury

Martin knew it was autumn again, for Dog ran into the house bringing wind and frost and a smell of apples turned to cider under trees. In dark clock-springs of hair, Dog fetched goldenrod, dust of farewell-summer, acorn-husk, hair of squirrel, feather of departed robin, sawdust from fresh-cut cordwood, and leaves like charcoals shaken from a blaze of maple trees. Dog jumped. Showers of brittle fern, blackberry vine, marsh-grass sprang over the bed where Martin shouted. No doubt, no doubt of it at all, this incredible beast was October!

'Here, boy, here!'

And Dog settled to warm Martin's body with all the bonfires and subtle burnings of the season, to fill the room with soft or heavy, wet or dry odours of far-travelling. In spring, he smelled of lilac, iris, lawn-mowered grass; in summer, ice-cream-moustached, he came pungent with firecracker, Roman candle, pinwheel, baked by the sun. But autumn! Autumn!

'Dog, what's it like outside?'

And lying there, Dog told as he always told. Lying there, Martin found autumn as in the old days before sickness bleached him white on his bed. Here was his contact, his carry-all, the quick-moving part of himself he sent with a yell to run and return, circle and scent, collect and deliver the time and texture of worlds in town, country, by creek, river, lake, down-cellar, up-attic, in closet or coal-bin. Ten dozen times a day he was gifted with sunflower seed, cinder-path, milkweed, horse-chestnut, or full flame-smell of pumpkin. Through the loomings of the universe Dog shuttled; the design was hid in his pelt. Put out your hand, it was there . . .

'And where did you go this morning?'

But he knew without hearing where Dog had rattled down hills where autumn lay in cereal crispness, where children lay in funeral pyres, in rustling heaps, the leaf-buried but watchful dead, as Dog and the world blew by.

Martin trembled his fingers, searched the thick fur, read the long journey. Through stubbled fields, over glitters of ravine creek, down marbled spread of cemetery yard, into woods. In the great season of spices and rare incense, now Martin ran through his emissary, around, about, and home!

The bedroom door opened.

'That dog of yours is in trouble again.'

Mother brought in a tray of fruit salad, cocoa, and toast, her blue eyes snapping.

'Mother . . .'

'Always digging places. Dug a hole in Miss Tarkin's garden this morning. She's spittin' mad. That's the fourth hole he's dug there this week.'

'Maybe he's looking for something.'

'Fiddlesticks, he's too darned curious. If he doesn't behave he'll be locked up.'

Martin looked at this woman as if she were a stranger.

'Oh, you wouldn't do that! How would I learn anything? How would I find things out if Dog didn't tell me?'

Mom's voice was quieter. 'Is that what he does – tell you things?'

'There's nothing I don't know when he goes out and around and back, *nothing* I can't find out from him!'

They both sat looking at Dog and the dry strewings of mould and seed over the quilt.

'Well, if he'll just stop digging where he shouldn't, he can run all he wants,' said Mother.

'Here, boy, here!'

And Martin snapped a tin note to the dog's collar:

MY OWNER IS MARTIN SMITH – TEN YEARS OLD – SICK IN BED – VISITORS WELCOME.

Dog barked. Mother opened the downstairs door and let him out.

Martin sat listening.

Far off and away you could hear Dog in the quiet autumn rain that was falling now. You could hear the barking-jingling fade, rise, fade again as he cut down alley, over lawn, to fetch back Mr Holloway and the oiled metallic smell of the delicate snowflake-interiored watches he repaired in his home shop. Or maybe he would bring Mr Jacobs, the grocer, whose clothes were rich with lettuce, celery, tomatoes, and the secret tinned and hidden smell of red demons stamped on cans of devilled ham. Mr Jacobs and his unseen pink-meat devils waved often from the yard below. Or Dog brought Mr Jackson, Mrs Gillespie, Mr Smith, Mrs Holmes, *any* friend or near-friend, encountered, cornered, begged, worried, and at last shepherded home for lunch, or tea-and-biscuits.

Now, listening, Martin heard Dog below, with footsteps moving in a light rain behind him. The downstairs bell rang. Mom opened the door, light voices murmured. Martin sat forward, face shining. The stair treads creaked. A young woman's voice laughed quietly. Miss Haight, of course, his teacher from school!

The bedroom door sprang open.

Martin had company.

Morning, afternoon, evening, dawn and dusk, sun and moon circled with Dog, who faithfully reported temperatures of turf and air, colour of earth and tree, consistency of mist or rain, but – most important of all – brought back again and again – Miss Haight.

On Saturday, Sunday and Monday she baked Martin

orange-iced cupcakes, brought him library books about dinosaurs and cavemen. On Tuesday, Wednesday and Thursday somehow he beat her at dominoes, somehow she lost at checkers, and soon, she cried, he'd defeat her handsomely at chess. On Friday, Saturday and Sunday they talked and never stopped talking, and she was so young and laughing and handsome and her hair was a soft, shining brown like the season outside the window, and she walked clear, clean and quick, a heartbeat warm in the bitter afternoon when he heard it. Above all, she had the secret of signs, and could read and interpret Dog and the symbols she searched out and plucked forth from his coat with her miraculous fingers. Eyes shut, softly laughing, in a gypsy's voice, she divined the world from the treasures in her hands.

And on Monday afternoon, Miss Haight was dead.

Martin sat up in bed, slowly.

'Dead?' he whispered.

Dead, said his mother, yes, dead, killed in an auto accident a mile out of town. Dead, yes, dead, which meant cold to Martin, which meant silence and whiteness and winter come long before its time. Dead, silent, cold, white. The thoughts circled round, blew down, and settled in whispers.

Martin held Dog, thinking; turned to the wall. The lady with the autumn-coloured hair. The lady with the laughter that was very gentle and never made fun and the eyes that watched your mouth to see everything you ever said. The-other-half-of-autumn-lady, who told what was left untold by Dog, about the world. The heartbeat at the still centre of grey afternoon. The heartbeat fading . . .

'Mom? What do they do in the graveyard, Mom, under the ground? Just lay there?'

'*Lie* there.'

'Lie there? Is that *all* they do? It doesn't sound like much fun.'

'For goodness' sake, it's not made out to be fun.'

'Why don't they jump up and run around once in a while if they get tired lying there? God's pretty silly –'

'Martin!'

'Well, you'd think He'd treat people better than to tell them to lie still for keeps. That's impossible. Nobody can do it! I tried once. Dog tries. I tell him, "dead Dog!" He plays dead awhile, then gets sick and tired and wags his tail or opens one eye and looks at me, bored. Boy, I bet sometimes those graveyard people do the same, huh, Dog?'

Dog barked.

'Be still with that kind of talk!' said Mother.

Martin looked off into space.

'Bet that's exactly what they do,' he said.

Autumn burnt the trees bare and ran Dog still farther around, fording creek, prowling graveyard as was his custom, and back in the dusk to fire off volleys of barking that shook windows wherever he turned.

In the late last days of October, Dog began to act as if the wind had changed and blew from a strange country. He stood quivering on the porch below. He whined, his eyes fixed at the empty land beyond town. He brought no visitors for Martin. He stood for hours each day, as if leashed, trembling, then shot away straight, as if someone had called. Each night, he returned later, with no one following. Each night, Martin sank deeper and deeper in his pillow.

'Well, people are busy,' said Mother. 'They haven't time

to notice the tag Dog carries. Or they mean to come visit, butforget.'

But there was more to it than that. There was the fevered shining in Dog's eyes, and his whimpering tic late at night, in some private dream. His shivering in the dark, under the bed. The way he sometimes stood half the night, looking at Martin as if some great and impossible secret was his and he knew no way to tell it save by savagely thumping his tail, or turning in endless circles, never to lie down, spinning and spinning again.

On October thirtieth, Dog ran out and didn't come back at all, even when after supper Martin heard his parents call and call. The hour grew late, the streets and sidewalks stood empty, the air moved cold about the house and there was nothing, nothing.

Long after midnight, Martin lay watching the world beyond the cool, clear glass windows. Now there was not even autumn, for there was no Dog to fetch it in. There would be no winter, for who could bring the snow to melt in your hands? Father, Mother? No, not the same. They couldn't play the game with its special secrets and rules, its sounds and pantomimes. No more seasons. No more time. The go-between, the emissary, was lost to the wild throngings of civilization, poisoned, stolen, hit by a car, left somewhere in a culvert . . .

Sobbing, Martin turned his face to his pillow. The world was a picture under glass, untouchable. The world was dead.

Martin twisted in bed and in three days the last Hallowe'en pumpkins were rotting in trash cans, papier-mâché skulls and witches were burnt on bonfires, and ghosts were stacked on shelves with other linens until next year.

To Martin, Hallowe'en had been nothing more than one evening when tin horns cried off in the cold autumn stars, children blew like goblin leaves along the flinty walks, flinging their heads, or cabbages, at porches, soap-writing names or similar magic symbols on icy windows. All of it as distant, unfathomable, and nightmarish as a puppet show seen from so many miles away that there is no sound or meaning.

For three days in November, Martin watched alternate light and shadow sift across his ceiling. The fire-pageant was over forever; autumn lay in cold ashes. Martin sank deeper, yet deeper in white marble layers of bed, motionless, listening always listening . . .

Friday evening, his parents kissed him good night and walked out of the house into the hushed cathedral weather toward a motion-picture show. Miss Tarkin from next door stayed on in the parlour below until Martin called down he was sleepy, then took her knitting off home.

In silence, Martin lay following the great move of stars down a clear and moonlit sky, remembering nights such as this when he'd spanned the town with Dog ahead, behind, around about, tracking the green-plush ravine, lapping slumbrous streams gone milky with the fullness of the moon, leaping cemetery tombstones while whispering the marble names; on, quickly on, through shaved meadows where the only motion was the off-on quivering of stars, to streets where shadows would not stand aside for you but crowded all the sidewalks for mile on mile. Run now run! Chasing, being chased by bitter smoke, fog, mist, wind, ghost of mind, fright of memory; home, safe, sound, snug-warm, asleep . . .

Nine o'clock.

Chime. The drowsy clock in the deep stairwell below. Chime.

Dog, come home, and run the world with you. Dog, bring a thistle with frost on it, or bring nothing else but the wind. Dog, where *are* you? Oh, listen, now, I'll call.

Martin held his breath.

Way off somewhere – a sound.

Martin rose up, trembling.

There, again – the sound.

So small a sound, like a sharp needle-point brushing the sky long miles and many miles away.

The dreamy echo of a dog – barking.

The sound of a dog crossing fields and farms, dirt roads and rabbit paths, running, running, letting out great barks of steam, cracking the night. The sound of a circling dog which came and went, lifted and faded, opened up, shut in, moved forward, went back, as if the animal were kept by someone on a fantastically long chain. As if the dog were running and someone whistled under the chestnut trees, in mould-shadow, tar-shadow, moon-shadow, walking, and the dog circled back and sprang out again towards home.

Dog! Martin thought, oh Dog, come home, boy! Listen, oh, listen, where you *been*? Come on, boy, make tracks!

Five, ten, fifteen minutes; near, very near, the bark, the sound. Martin cried out, thrust his feet from the bed, leaned to the window. Dog! Listen, boy! Dog! Dog! He said it over and over. Dog! Dog! Wicked Dog, run off and gone all these days! Bad Dog, good Dog, home, boy, hurry, and bring what you can!

Near now, near, up the street, barking, to knock clapboard housefronts with sound, whirl iron cocks on rooftops in the moon, firing off volleys – Dog! now at the door below . . .

Martin shivered.

Should he run – let Dog in, or wait for Mom and Dad? Wait? Oh, God, wait? But what if Dog ran off again? No, he'd go down, snatch the door wide, yell, grab Dog in, and run upstairs so fast, laughing, crying, holding tight, that . . .

Dog stopped barking.

Hey! Martin almost broke the window, jerking to it.

Silence. As if someone had told Dog to hush now, hush, hush.

A full minute passed. Martin clenched his fists.

Below, a faint whimpering.

Then, slowly, the downstairs front door opened. Someone was kind enough to have opened the door for Dog. Of course! Dog had brought Mr Jacobs or Mr Gillespie or Miss Tarkin, or . . .

The downstairs door shut.

Dog raced upstairs, whining, flung himself on the bed.

'Dog, Dog, where've you *been*, what've you *done*! Dog, Dog!'

And he crushed Dog hard and long to himself, weeping. Dog, Dog. He laughed and shouted. Dog! But after a moment he stopped laughing and crying, suddenly.

He pulled away. He held the animal and looked at him, eyes widening.

The odour coming from Dog was different.

It was a smell of strange earth. It was a smell of night within night, the smell of digging down deep in shadow through earth that had lain cheek by jowl with things that were long hidden and decayed. A stinking and rancid soil fell away in clods of dissolution from Dog's muzzle and paws. He had dug deep. He had dug very deep indeed. That *was* it, wasn't it? wasn't it? *wasn't* it!

What kind of message was this from Dog? What could such a message mean? The stench – the ripe and awful cemetery earth.

Dog was a bad dog, digging where he shouldn't. Dog was a good dog, always making friends. Dog loved people. Dog brought them home.

And now, moving up the dark hall stairs, at intervals, came the sound of feet, one foot dragged after the other, painfully, slowly, slowly, slowly.

Dog shivered. A rain of strange night earth fell seething on the bed.

Dog turned.

The bedroom door whispered in.

Martin had company.

The Lamp

Agatha Christie

It was undoubtedly an old house. The whole square was old, with that disapproving dignified old age often met with in a cathedral town. But No. 19 gave the impression of an elder among elders; it had a veritable patriarchal solemnity; it towered greyest of the grey, haughtiest of the haughty, chillest of the chill. Austere, forbidding, and stamped with that particular desolation attaching to all houses that have been long untenanted, it reigned above the other dwellings.

In any other town it would have been freely labelled 'haunted', but Weyminster was averse from ghosts and considered them hardly respectable except as the appanage of a 'county family'. So No. 19 was never alluded to as a haunted house; but nevertheless it remained, year after year, 'To be Let or Sold'.

Mrs Lancaster looked at the house with approval as she drove up with the talkative house agent, who was in an unusually hilarious mood at the idea of getting No. 19 off his books. He inserted the key in the door without ceasing his appreciative comments.

'How long has the house been empty?' inquired Mrs Lancaster, cutting short his flow of language rather brusquely.

Mr Raddish (of Raddish & Foplow) became slightly confused.

'Er – er – some time,' he remarked blandly.

'So I should think,' said Mrs Lancaster drily.

The dimly lighted hall was chill with a sinister chill. A more imaginative woman might have shivered, but this woman happened to be eminently practical. She was tall with much dark brown hair just tinged with grey and rather cold blue eyes.

She went over the house from attic to cellar, asking a pertinent question from time to time. The inspection over, she came back into one of the front rooms looking out on the square and faced the agent with a resolute mien.

'What is the matter with the house?'

Mr Raddish was taken by surprise.

'Of course, an unfurnished house is always a little gloomy,' he parried feebly.

'Nonsense,' said Mrs Lancaster. 'The rent is ridiculously low for such a house – purely nominal. There must be some reason for it. I suppose the house is haunted?'

Mr Raddish gave a nervous little start but said nothing.

Mrs Lancaster eyed him keenly. After a few moments she spoke again.

'Of course that is all nonsense. I don't believe in ghosts or anything of that sort, and personally it is no deterrent to my taking the house; but servants, unfortunately, are very credulous and easily frightened. It would be kind of you to tell me exactly what – what thing *is* supposed to haunt this place.'

'I – er – really don't know,' stammered the house agent.

'I am sure you must,' said the lady quietly. 'I cannot take

TO BE
LET
OR

the house without knowing. What was it? A murder?'

'Oh! no,' cried Mr Raddish, shocked by the idea of anything so alien to the respectability of the square. 'It's – it's – only a child.'

'A child?'

'Yes.

'I don't know the story exactly,' he continued reluctantly. 'Of course, there are all kinds of different versions, but I believe that about thirty years ago a man going by the name of Williams took No. 19. Nothing was known of him; he kept no servants; he had no friends; he seldom went out in the daytime. He had one child, a little boy. After he had been there about two months, he went up to London, and had barely set foot in the metropolis before he was recognized as being a man 'wanted' by the police on some charge – exactly what, I do not know. But it must have been a grave one, because, sooner than give himself up, he shot himself. Meanwhile, the child lived on here, alone in the house. He had food for a little time, and he waited day after day for his father's return. Unfortunately, it had been impressed upon him that he was never under any circumstances to go out of the house or to speak to anyone. He was a weak, ailing, little creature, and did not dream of disobeying this command. In the night, the neighbours, not knowing that his father had gone away, often heard him sobbing in the awful loneliness and desolation of the empty house.'

Mr Raddish paused.

'And – er – the child starved to death,' he concluded, in the same tones as he might have announced that it had just begun to rain.

'And it is the child's ghost that is supposed to haunt the place?' asked Mrs Lancaster.

'It is nothing of consequence really,' Mr Raddish hastened to assure her. 'There's nothing *seen*, not *seen*, only people say, ridiculous, of course, but they do say they hear – the child – crying, you know.'

Mrs Lancaster moved towards the front door.

'I like the house very much,' she said. 'I shall get nothing as good for the price. I will think it over and let you know.'

'It really looks very cheerful, doesn't it, Papa?'

Mrs Lancaster surveyed her new domain with approval. Gay rugs, well-polished furniture, and many knick-knacks, had quite transformed the gloomy aspect of No. 19.

She spoke to a thin, bent old man with stooping shoulders and a delicate mystical face. Mr Winburn did not resemble his daughter; indeed no greater contrast could be imagined than that presented by her resolute practicalness and his dreamy abstraction.

'Yes,' he answered with a smile, 'no one would dream the house was haunted.'

'Papa, don't talk nonsense! On our first day too.'

Mr Winburn smiled.

'Very well, my dear, we will agree that there are no such things as ghosts.'

'And please,' continued Mrs Lancaster, 'don't say a word before Geoff. He's so imaginative.'

Geoff was Mrs Lancaster's little boy. The family consisted of Mr Winburn, his widowed daughter, and Geoffrey.

Rain had begun to beat against the window – pitter-patter, pitter-patter.

'Listen,' said Mr Winburn. 'Is it not like little footsteps?'

'It's more like rain,' said Mrs Lancaster, with a smile.

'But *that*, *that* is a footstep,' cried her father, bending forward to listen.

Mrs Lancaster laughed outright.

'That's Geoff coming downstairs.'

Mr Winburn was obliged to laugh too. They were having tea in the hall, and he had been sitting with his back to the staircase. He now turned his chair round to face it.

Little Geoffrey was coming down, rather slowly and sedately, with a child's awe of a strange place. The stairs were of polished oak, uncarpeted. He came across and stood by his mother. Mr Winburn gave a slight start. As the child was crossing the floor, he distinctly heard another pair of footsteps on the stairs, as of someone following Geoffrey. Dragging footsteps, curiously painful they were. Then he shrugged his shoulders incredulously. 'The rain, no doubt,' he thought.

'I'm looking at the spongecakes,' remarked Geoff with the admirably detached air of one who points out an interesting fact.

His mother hastened to comply with the hint.

'Well, Sonny, how do you like your new home?' she asked.

'Lots,' replied Geoffrey with his mouth generously filled. 'Pounds and pounds and pounds.' After this last assertion, which was evidently expressive of the deepest contentment, he relapsed into silence, only anxious to remove the spongecake from the sight of man in the least time possible.

Having bolted the last mouthful, he burst forth into speech.

'Oh! Mummy, there's attics here, Jane says; and can I go at once and *eggz*plore them? And there might be a secret door. Jane says there isn't, but I think there must be, and, anyhow, I know there'll be *pipes*, *water pipes* (with a face full of ecstasy) and can I play with them, and, oh! can I go and see the boi-i-ler?' He spun out the last word with such evident rapture that his grandfather felt ashamed to reflect that this peerless delight of childhood only conjured up to his imagination the picture of hot water that wasn't hot, and heavy and numerous plumber's bills.

'We'll see about the attics tomorrow, darling,' said Mrs Lancaster. 'Suppose you fetch your bricks and build a nice house, or an engine.'

'Don't want to build an 'ouse.'

'*H*ouse.'

'House, or h'engine h'either.'

'Build a boiler,' suggested his grandfather.

Geoffrey brightened.

'With pipes?'

'Yes, lots of pipes.'

Geoffrey ran away happily to fetch his bricks.

The rain was still falling. Mr Winburn listened. Yes, it must have been the rain he had heard; but it did sound like footsteps.

He had a queer dream that night.

He dreamt that he was walking through a town, a great city it seemed to him. But it was a children's city; there were no grown-up people there, nothing but children, crowds of them. In his dream they all rushed to the stranger crying: 'Have you brought him?' It seemed that he understood what they meant and shook his head sadly. When they saw this, the children turned away and began to cry, sobbing bitterly.

The city and the children faded away and he awoke to find himself in bed, but the sobbing was still in his ears. Though wide awake, he heard it distinctly; and he remembered that Geoffrey slept on the floor below, while this sound of a child's sorrow descended from above. He sat up and struck a match. Instantly the sobbing ceased.

Mr Winburn did not tell his daughter of the dream or its sequel. That it was no trick of his imagination, he was convinced; indeed soon afterwards he heard it again in the daytime. The wind was howling in the chimney, but *this* was a separate sound – distinct, unmistakable: pitiful little heartbroken sobs.

He found out too that he was not the only one to hear them. He overheard the housemaid saying to the parlourmaid that she 'didn't think as that there nurse was kind to Master Geoffrey. She'd 'eard 'im crying 'is little 'eart out only that very morning.' Geoffrey had come down to breakfast and lunch beaming with health and happiness; and Mr Winburn knew that it was not Geoff who had been crying, but that other child whose dragging footsteps had startled him more than once.

Mrs Lancaster alone never heard anything. Her ears were not perhaps attuned to catch sounds from another world.

Yet one day she also received a shock.

'Mummy,' said Geoffrey plaintively. 'I wish you'd let me play with that little boy.'

Mrs Lancaster looked up from her writing table with a smile.

'What little boy, dear?'

'I don't know his name. He was in an attic, sitting on the floor crying, but he ran away when he saw me. I suppose he was *shy* (with slight contempt), not like a *big* boy, and then, when I was in the nursery building, I saw him standing in the door watching me build, and he looked so awful lonely and as though he wanted to play wiv me. I said: "Come and build a h'engine," but he didn't say nothing, just looked as – as though he saw a lot of chocolates, and his mummy had told him not to touch them.' Geoff sighed, sad personal reminiscences evidently recurring to him. 'But when I asked Jane who he was and told her I wanted to play wiv him, she said there wasn't no little boy in the 'ouse and not to tell naughty stories. I don't love Jane at all.'

Mrs Lancaster got up.

'Jane was right. There was no little boy.'

'But I saw him. Oh! Mummy, do let me play wiv him, he did look so awful lonely and unhappy. I *do* want to do something to "make him better".'

Mrs Lancaster was about to speak again, but her father shook his head.

'Geoff,' he said very gently, 'that poor little boy *is* lonely, and perhaps you may do something to comfort him; but you must find out how by yourself – like a puzzle – do you see?'

'Is it because I am getting *big* I must do it all my lone?'

'Yes, because you are getting big.'

As the boy left the room, Mrs Lancaster turned to her father impatiently.

'Papa, this is absurd. To encourage the boy to believe the servants' idle tales!'

'No servant has told the child anything,' said the old man gently. 'He's seen – what I *hear*, what I could see perhaps if I were his age.'

'But it's such nonsense! Why don't I see it or hear it?'

Mr Winburn smiled, a curiously tired smile, but did not reply.

'Why?' repeated his daughter. 'And why did you tell him he could help the – the – thing? It's – it's all so impossible.'

The old man looked at her with his thoughtful glance.

'Why not?' he said. 'Do you remember these words:

> What Lamp has Destiny to guide
> Her little Children stumbling in the Dark?
> "A Blind Understanding," Heaven replied.

'Geoffrey has that – a blind understanding. All children possess it. It is only as we grow older that we lose it, that we cast it away from us. Sometimes, when we are quite old, a faint gleam comes back to us, but the Lamp burns brightest in childhood. That is why I think Geoffrey may help.'

'I don't understand,' murmured Mrs Lancaster feebly.

'No more do I. That – that child is in trouble and wants – to be set free. But how? I do not know, but – it's awful to think of it – sobbing its heart out – a *child*.'

A month after this conversation Geoffrey fell very ill. The east wind had been severe, and he was not a strong child. The doctor shook his head and said that it was a grave case. To Mr Winburn he divulged more and confessed that the case was quite hopeless. 'The child would never have lived to grow up, under any circumstances,' he added.

'There has been serious lung trouble for a long time.'

It was when nursing Geoff that Mrs Lancaster became aware of that – other child. At first the sobs were an indistinguishable part of the wind, but gradually they became more distinct, more unmistakable. Finally she heard them in moments of dead calm: a child's sobs – dull, hopeless, heartbroken.

Geoff grew steadily worse and in his delirium he spoke of the 'little boy' again and again. 'I do want to help him get away, I do!' he cried.

Succeeding the delirium there came a state of lethargy. Geoffrey lay very still, hardly breathing, sunk in oblivion. There was nothing to do but wait and watch. Then there came a still night, clear and calm, without one breath of wind.

Suddenly the child stirred. His eyes opened. He looked past his mother towards the open door. He tried to speak and she bent down to catch the half-breathed words.

'All right, I'm comin',' he whispered; then he sank back.

The mother felt suddenly terrified; she crossed the room to her father. Somewhere near them the other child was laughing. Joyful, contented, triumphant, the silvery laughter echoed through the room.

'I'm frightened; I'm frightened,' she moaned.

He put his arm round her protectingly. A sudden gust of wind made them both start, but it passed swiftly and left the air quiet as before.

The laughter had ceased and there crept to them a faint sound, so faint as hardly to be heard, but growing louder till they could distinguish it. Footsteps – light footsteps, swiftly departing.

Pitter-patter, pitter-patter, they ran – those well-known halting little feet. Yet – surely – now *other* footsteps suddenly mingled with them, moving with a quicker and a lighter tread.

With one accord they hastened to the door.

Down, down, down, past the door, close to them, pitter-patter, pitter-patter, went the unseen feet of the little children *together*.

Mrs Lancaster looked up wildly.

'There are *two* of them – *two*!'

Grey with sudden fear, she turned towards the cot in the

corner, but her father restrained her gently, and pointed away.

'There,' he said simply.

Pitter-patter, pitter-patter – fainter and fainter.

And then – silence.

We'll Always Have Tommy

Brian Morse

Saturday afternoon, after lunch, the two Browns went to visit his grave. It wasn't far to walk and they didn't take the car which had too many unpleasant memories lingering about it – particularly about the dashboard where there had been blood.

They put the flowers which Mrs Brown had picked from the hedgerow on the tombstone, then stood in silence, and after a little Mr Brown started weeping. His wife stood and listened to the hard, dry sobs that racked the man.

'I shouldn't have!' he cried. 'I shouldn't have! My son! My son!'

It was torture. Mrs Brown almost put her arms around him, anything to stop it. But to be honest she couldn't bear his touch. The nursing after he came out of hospital had been agony, all that lifting and pulling and shoving his helpless body.

Tentatively she touched the back of his hand to show her sympathy. 'Time heals all things,' she murmured. The Vicar had said that. Blindly Mr Brown turned her hand about and gave it a squeeze expressive of ultimate grief. She wrenched away.

'We'll always have Tommy,' she said. 'Nothing can change that.'

Later they walked back. It was striking three from somewhere across town as they turned into the Avenue.

'Better change my things and get out on that garden,' said Mr Brown, who since the accident had been besotted with grief.

Mrs Brown was watching the neighbours' curtains. 'There they go,' she could hear them whispering. 'Poor man! It's the first time he's been down there. He couldn't bear the idea of Tommy underground, those two were so close. But *her*! She could never do anything with him.'

She realized her husband was speaking.

'I said, when I'm really better I'll see to selling that car.'

They went in through the gate. 'But we've got to learn to live without him. There's some things you've got to try and forget.'

He knew at once it was something he shouldn't have said.

I

Nearer teatime Mr Brown came in from the garden. He'd worked himself to a standstill, it had been much too soon after the accident to pitch into work like that. But it was pleasant in a way, his body aching. His thoughts turned into more pleasant channels. He might have whistled, except he thought at once of Tommy dead. But without him, or with him, life had to go on. He resolved to put by morbid thoughts, to begin anew.

Then, as he passed the sitting-room, he glanced in at the window and stopped short. And stared. It was incredible. For a split second he was overcome with remorse. Tommy! Forgive me!

But it was a trick of the light.

Still he came in pale. 'I could have sworn I knew that face,' he said more to himself than to anyone else.

'Whose face?' his wife asked.

'A lad's curled up in the sofa.'

'What lad? What are you talking about?'

'A lad curled up in the sofa. I saw him through the window. Oh, it's all right. There's no need to go rushing in. It was only a trick of the light. But it gave me a shock. Hey! Where are you going?'

'To have a look!'

'What do you expect to find?'

But Mrs Brown hadn't bothered to listen.

And she seemed to be gone a terribly long time. He was just beginning to wonder if anything was wrong when she came back.

'You don't know *him*,' she said, detaching a stray hair from her jumper. 'And he's dog-tired. Don't wake him.'

'There is someone! Who?' He half got up.

She swallowed hard. 'A little boy from down the road,' she said. 'His mamma goes to church. He brought me a message. Poor little scrap! He must have crept in there for a sleep.'

She couldn't look straight at her husband.

'For a minute I could have sworn it was Tommy,' said Mr Brown who'd been given a second shock. 'When he was younger.' He looked grey and ill.

'When he was eight,' said Mrs Brown.

'Eh?'

'When he was eight,' she repeated as if she wished she hadn't said it. Then she said more briskly, 'Now, remember, don't wake him.'

'Don't wake him?'

'You heard me. And wash your hands.'

He didn't move. 'I always think of Tommy that age,' he said.

Later, washed and brushed, Mr Brown went into the lounge on tiptoe. All the same the boy woke up. Or perhaps he was just pretending to be asleep. Anyway he yawned, though very politely, and put his hand in front of his mouth, and peeped out of the corner of his eye at whoever had arrived.

'Don't mind if I have the telly, do you?' Mr Brown asked, even if it was his own sitting-room. 'I like to Saturdays.'

It was the wrestling. Al Capone against Krupp the Kitten.

Mr Brown was puzzled and kept glancing sideways. The boy didn't seem to be interested in the telly. There was no reason for him to stay. And the resemblance was incredible.

He took advantage of the second commercial break. 'You remind me of someone. Very strongly you do. Even the way you yawn reminds me.'

The boy perched on the very edge of his chair, and seemed to be waiting for Mr Brown to say more; but he didn't.

They lapsed into silence.

Then, during the fifth round of Al Capone against Krupp the Kitten, he yawned again. Mr Brown looked as if he might cry. He pulled out a paper handkerchief and dabbed at a tear that had gathered in the corner of his eye.

'How can I ever forget?' he said. 'My fault ... that lorry ...'

Suddenly he saw through a veil of tears that the boy was standing in front of him. 'Never mind me, son,' he said. 'Are you going home? Perhaps you better. I don't feel very well.'

The boy didn't answer. Perhaps he was just upset at the sight of an adult crying. He stood there.

'You don't want to sit on my knee, do you?' Mr Brown said doubtfully. He'd pulled himself together a bit. 'You're rather old for that.'

The two looked at one another, and the boy swung his head in a way that could have meant yes or no, and looked back at Mr Brown.

'You better be running along. Your mother will be expecting you. She'll be sending your father after you.'

'Father?' said the boy.

'Yes! Father!' said Mr Brown rather crossly. 'Your father will be looking for you.'

He raised himself up and stood staring at Tommy's photo on top of the telly while he slowly turned the knob to 'Off'.

When he looked round the boy had gone.

Mr Brown went back to work the week after. As was only natural that first day he came back dog-tired. Over his meal he said to his wife, 'You know, I think I'll have to use that car tomorrow. There's no reason why I shouldn't.'

'The car! You've got no heart! How could you?'

'Just till I get time to get round to selling it,' he snapped. Then he frowned. 'You know Tommy was fond of that car. We had it almost as long as him. He could have been learning in two or three years' time.'

While he was washing and shaving after his meal Mrs Brown moped in the kitchen. Then there was a knock at the door, very low. She hurriedly pulled and patted her hair into shape at the little mirror that was hung over the sink and opened up.

'Oh, it's you!' she said.

When her husband came down he found the boy in the kitchen.

'How do you do?' he said in his most jovial fashion. He had a way with kids.

This boy he couldn't keep his eyes off. He had made him

think. The boy followed him out to the garage and hung around while he tinkered about with the engine.

'Do you want to play with the steering-wheel?' Mr Brown asked.

The boy shook his head. He wouldn't say a word, he just hung around.

'Have you got lots of friends?' asked Mr Brown.

The boy shook his head.

'Do your parents give you lots of presents?'

He even shook his head to that.

'Well, some of us won't be helped,' said Mr Brown.

He didn't notice exactly when the boy left.

It was almost dark when he came back in. 'Another message?' he asked his wife.

'What?'

'That boy. Another message?'

'Oh, a message! Yes!'

He cleared his throat as if he was going to make a speech. 'I've been thinking,' he said, 'while I was out in the garage.'

Mrs Brown went over to look out at the dusk.

'I know what you'll think, but that boy's given me an idea. It's the resemblance to Tommy. We're still young enough to adopt some kid, give him a good home, if we don't have another ourselves. Be doing a service to us both. I like a kid about the house.'

She stared out of the window until the silence was unbearable. Then she turned round and gave him an unfathomable look.

'The one we've got's enough,' she said. 'You seem intent on hammering more nails into Tommy's coffin.'

Mr Brown left it at that.

The next time Mr Brown saw the boy was the following Saturday.

By now Mr Brown was looking bronzed and fit. Everyone said, 'He's made a miraculous recovery, considering . . .' He would joke with the neighbours over the garden fence, and his wife would watch him from her kitchen window, a cup poised between draining board and sink, watching him with a far-away look that seemed to see something else besides.

That Saturday, when he came in, Mr Brown said, 'I'll never forget what you said that day we went down to the cemetery: "We'll always have Tommy." Sometimes out there on the garden I have only to shut my eyes and I can feel him there beside me. I know it's silly, but whatever happens he'll always be ours.'

'I asked that little boy to stay to tea,' Mrs Brown said very quickly and got on with what she was doing.

To judge by the size of the meal it was a special event. 'She knows what we like,' Mr Brown said to their visitor who had materialized in the front room. 'We haven't had a meal like this in ages. You ought to come again.' He tucked in with vigour. 'A real good meal. But why in the best room?'

'You don't remember?' Mrs Brown asked.

'Remember?'

'If you don't remember it's not worth telling you.'

'Now, come on! Tell me!'

'No, I won't!'

He racked his brains and then did remember: it almost choked him. It was Tommy's birthday.

He looked across at his wife. Her eyes were brimming

with tears. 'Oh, I'm sorry,' he said. 'How could I?'

If only that damn boy hadn't been there he could have been more affectionate.

For the rest of the evening he made a special effort to be nice. He cleared away the things, he washed up, he wouldn't let her lift a finger.

About bedtime, a boy's bedtime (but Mr Brown had gone to bed early since the accident and did so still), Mr Brown stretched and said, 'Some of us ought to be getting to bed.' He looked at the boy especially.

'It is tiring,' agreed Mrs Brown. She got up and went to the kitchen and left the two alone.

'I'm tired, too,' the boy said with that secret smile on his face Mrs Brown loved so much.

'Won't your mother be expecting you?' Mr Brown asked. 'We don't want her out looking for you.'

The boy replied almost unwillingly, 'She knows where I am. Anyhow I trust her.'

'Trust *her*!' That seemed a queer expression to Mr Brown. But he didn't pursue the thought, he wasn't really attending to the boy. He was watching instead the stooped figure of his wife in the kitchen. 'Well, good night!' he called. 'I'm tired. It was all that gardening. Make sure the lights are out. The front door's on the chain. I'm off. Upstairs.'

But he didn't move. He just stood there, rubbing at his sideboards Mrs Brown had once been so enamoured of.

She felt his eyes on her, and the eyes, too, of the boy. She knew what was wanted.

She turned and looked straight up at her husband, something she hadn't done for months. And he looked back and smiled. How far apart they'd been! For a moment there might have been no one else there, they were so private and alone. (Indeed, glancing in the mirror, Mrs Brown would have only seen herself and her husband.)

'Can he stay? Just for the night?' she said very low. 'Just one night?'

But Mr Brown didn't seem to have heard her, or perhaps he thought she said something else, or perhaps she didn't really say it at all, for *he* said without taking his eyes away from hers, 'I hope I wasn't rude to him. That boy seems to have nipped off. You'll be straight up, Mother?'

'Yes, Father,' she said, wringing her hands. 'I'll be up. As soon as I can.'

Then a terrible thing happened. The boy ran at Mr Brown crying, 'Father! Father! Don't you remember me, Father?'

But all he achieved was to run straight through him.

And the boy wouldn't be convinced. 'Father! Father!' he shouted, and Mrs Brown covered her ears while her husband looked on with amazement.

Then he screamed at his mother, 'He can't see me! He can't see me! It's your fault! It's your fault! You never told him I'd come!'

Mrs Brown couldn't help it, she screamed back, 'It's not my fault! It's not! It was him! He did it! And *then* he never saw you! I tried to tell him! I did!'

'What are you shouting about?' said Mr Brown in more amazement. 'What fault? What him? Are you still going on about that? There's no one else here, is there?'

And then Tommy was gone. And Mr Brown was running for the neighbours.

2

For eight years after that Mrs Brown lived in two worlds, although she was happy in neither.

For Tommy did come back again, this time for good, but this time he hardly, if ever, bothered his father: it was his mother he'd come to live with. She took this as a sign that he knew who loved and wanted him most, certainly she was glad that only she, and no one else, possessed him. But there was a dark look in Tommy's eyes which Mrs Brown had to force herself to forget.

She didn't think anyone found out, though once the next-door neighbour asked, 'Who you got staying? I heard you talking to someone – or was you singing?'

Mrs Brown went even more carefully after that.

And then her husband.

At first Tommy's coming back had helped – happy with one, happy with both – but later Tommy began to make more and more demands on her time and affection, and her husband began (it seemed to her) to become more and more callous about their son.

For instance, he went on and on about adoption, although he knew what she felt about that. Or he would say things like, 'Tommy would be twenty-one by now. Did you see that girl he was so soft on got married last week?' And once he suggested renting out Tommy's bedroom to help pay for, of all things, a new car. He never did get round to that.

Tommy, too, disturbed her. He was growing fast – nine, ten, eleven, twelve – and he seemed to have the knowledge of two. It didn't make him any nicer to her, though you would have thought it might since she'd proved twice over that she was the one who loved him most. Still, she consoled herself, as she had before, kids that age were all over their fathers. It was only natural. But he would go away and sulk for hours on end, and by the time he was thirteen he would disappear for days although he knew it worried her stiff. And sometimes, much later, he would be vicious and walk straight through his father, which always gave Mr Brown a headache and made him nasty to his wife.

Mrs Brown could see they were heading for disaster, in fact she secretly thought that both her son and her husband were actually preparing for one.

One day her husband did go too far. During an argument (Tommy, who was eleven, was sitting in the corner – it was as if his father *knew* that) he shouted at her, 'It's you needs to see a doctor again! Who'll ever forget that time you were screaming at thin air? You're haunted by that dead boy!'

And Tommy laughed!

From that moment Mrs Brown knew she was living it all once again. Once again her husband was going to murder her son, and Tommy was willing him on just to spite her. Every glance, every word of her husband seemed to betray his intentions. However much she tried to convince herself of the opposite, even though she knew her husband couldn't see Tommy, she was sure that somehow he was going to kill her son.

By the time Tommy was fifteen again, Mrs Brown was a respectable, greying, middle-aged woman whom men would still sometimes look at twice in the street. But slightly dotty, people said. She was lucky she had such an easy-going husband.

And what her husband had to put up with! A wife who would hardly move out of the house except to meet out of school a son she no longer had; who spent all day moping around the home, not getting anything done, and would be up half the night 'catching up' and peeping into her dead son's bedroom every half an hour (she still kept the bedroom warm and aired for when he deigned to sleep there); a wife who neither seemed to hear nor care what her husband said or did except when it concerned that dead son; who still set the table for three, and religiously celebrated a meaningless birthday . . .

People seeing her standing at the window would wave, but she never saw them. Once people had liked her. Perhaps they still did. But in the end they gave up waving.

3

Eight years had passed, eight difficult years for Mr Brown. Sometimes he was surprised at the intensity with which his wife remembered, sometimes he was shocked, sometimes he cursed it for ruining their life. Though he always suppressed the last thought which gave him a pang of guilt. Perhaps he hadn't been *altogether* loyal.

But one morning – it was the anniversary of Tommy's death – he'd noticed the date on the paper – he said, 'Tommy might be raising a family himself now. I see that girl he was going about with's just had twins.'

His wife knew exactly what he was leading up to. That

and the fact she hadn't seen Tommy for over six weeks made her want to scream.

But Mr Brown felt he had to have it out once and for all, so later on he said, 'I'm sorry to keep on about it, but it's not too late to think of adopting some little child. Otherwise we'll be getting past it soon. What do you think? I've got some literature on the subject.'

'I won't listen,' she said. 'We've still got Tommy.'

He felt himself boiling over. 'Tommy!' he cried. 'We *had* Tommy! What's Tommy to you now? You two never got on even though you were always smarming over him. You make me hate Tommy! For eight years he's plagued me!'

'That's not true!' Mrs Brown screamed. 'That's not true!'

'You're mad!' Mr Brown shouted. 'He's always coming between us! I wish he were dead!'

He must have grown confused.

They were both so upset that he went away to the pub for the whole of dinner.

But in the afternoon he came running in, delirious with excitement.

'I've seen him!' he shouted. 'I've seen him!'

'Who?' said Mrs Brown, who didn't care what he had or hadn't seen.

'Tommy!'

'You!'

'He was in the road, but he ran away!'

'Tommy! *You* saw him?'

'Come on!' he shouted. 'I'm going to get the car out.'

'But he's dead, despite your threats.' It was she who was confused now. 'You never saw him before.'

He didn't hear her. He rushed and backed the car out.

Mrs Brown rushed out too and wrung her hands in her apron.

'He's been here all the time, but you never realized. Why should you see him now?'

For answer he only ran round and pushed her into the passenger seat and started off. He'd forgotten Tommy was dead. 'We'll catch him,' he said. 'He can't have gone far. You can see down all the side-streets.'

They drove down the Avenue and went right into the main road. They just missed a bus as they turned. Mr Brown was talking fast and sometimes none too clearly. He'd had a bit too much to drink. 'I was just thinking of what I said – "I wish he were dead" – and really missing Tommy, than who should I see –'

'No! Not you!' cried his wife.

'Shut up!' shouted Mr Brown. 'You were the one who was all over him. You were the one who came between us, alive or dead. You're not keeping us apart now.'

There was a figure on the right-hand side walking away from them that looked like Tommy. But he was moving fast. Luckily there was little traffic. Mr Brown speeded.

'Look! He's stopped! He knows I'm coming,' shouted Mr Brown. He was doing forty.

'He came for me,' she said, 'not for you. I've looked after him these last eight years. It was you that spurned him when it came to the test.'

The figure had stopped, and now they were so near Mrs Brown had to cover her eyes. The figure turned round.

'It is Tommy!' said Mr Brown.

His wife uncovered her eyes.

Then the figure stepped off the pavement, although they

didn't seem to be getting any nearer, and walked into the road, and Mrs Brown looked up and cried, 'Tommy! It *was* him you came back for!' and suddenly – Mr Brown didn't know how – Tommy was five yards in front of them and they were still doing forty and his wife was wrenching at the wheel to save her son, to save someone and –

It was an almost exact replica of the previous accident, except this time it wasn't Mr Brown who had wrenched the wheel away from the oncoming tanker and so saved himself and not his passenger.

His wife was smashed beyond recognition against the lamp-post.

Mr Brown was vaguely aware of Tommy speaking before he lapsed into unconsciousness.

'I don't blame you, Father, even if you did choose yourself,' he was saying. 'Even so I loved you best. Now we can really be together.'

Dead Trouble

Aidan Chambers

The trouble with being dead is that no one believes you are alive. Things were different years ago. Or so I'm told by others better able to know than myself. In earlier times people still believed in God and the Devil, and therefore, of course, in ghosts. But nowadays all that has changed.

Only last week, for instance, one of the oldest inhabitants in these parts made a chilling appearance at a party where the guests were playing Ouija. But instead of being received with shocked horror, he was laughed at. Imagine it! The guests laughed and said he wasn't there at all, that they had all had too much to drink, which, along with the Ouija, had affected their imaginations, making them *think* they saw a ghost. My own experiences in the last few months, since I was forced to take up this way of life, have been pretty humiliating, but this treatment of an expert, senior ghost, a professional you might say, was a scandal. People here talked about it for days, and the poor fellow himself was so upset he spent every night for weeks afterwards lying around sulking invisibly. And I don't blame him; the whole business was dispiriting.

But I'd better begin at the beginning, otherwise I'll never get to the purpose of this message.

Three months ago I fell into the concrete-mixer at work. The mixer was a huge affair, not one of those little ones you see churning away on small building sites. We made bulk concrete in it, ready for transporting in large quantities by truck to major constructions. At any rate, I fell in. I blame myself really; it was no one else's fault. I should have kept my mind on my work instead of thinking about Veronica. (She was my girl-friend at the time, and was being a bit troublesome.)

Before I go on, I must explain that death is quite different viewed from my present situation than it is viewed from yours. As with most things in life – or after it, come to that – death does not seem half so bad when it is all over as you think it is going to be before it happens. Just like going to the dentist is worse to think about beforehand than it is when you get there, and is often quite a laugh afterwards. Well, dying is just the same; we here are always laughing about it, especially when people have just arrived – it is such a relief to them, and they wonder what all the fuss was about.

Like so many 'modern' people, I used to think death meant the end of everything. Blackout. Kaput. The finish. Needless to say, I know differently now. (Mind you, there have been times during the last few months when I have wished my death really had been the end!)

Death is like everything else in another way too. Some people die lucky; others don't. I didn't. Though up till my death I had been pretty fortunate, the episode with the concrete-mixer seemed to change all that. I haven't had a stroke of luck since.

Let me explain.

When I slipped into the mixer, I was on my own. My mate Harry was having his tea-break; I was keeping things going until he returned to relieve me. But when he got back I had gone. He isn't particularly bright, isn't Harry, and he didn't think of looking in the mixer for me. He thought I'd gone off sick.

At home, my family (father, mother, sister) started worrying when I didn't get in that night. But they waited until the following morning before they informed the police. After a bit of investigating, everyone decided I must have run off, and the police put me on the missing persons list.

Meanwhile, of course, I had been churning round with the half-mixed concrete. I hadn't expected to fall in so I escaped the awful business of knowing I was going to die, though as it turned out, it wasn't such an ordeal as you might suppose. For a start, it was over quickly. A slip of the foot, a nasty couple of minutes swilling about with the sand and gravel and cement and water, and I was dead. (I didn't much care for the gravel – I've always had a fairly sensitive skin – but the change of state from what I was to what I am now happened in the blink of an eye, and was really rather a pleasant sensation. Like sliding into sleep.)

My death having happened, I was in a position to watch developments without feeling a thing. Or, to put it more accurately, without feeling anything that was being done to my 'mortal remains': my corpse.

When Harry got back from his tea-break, he transferred the load of mixed concrete into a truck, and as my remains were by then well mixed with the concrete, they were transferred to the truck too. The truck drove off to a building site in central Manchester, and there the load of concrete (and my corpse) was poured straight into a mould for a stanchion that was to be used as one of the main supports of a new office block.

And there my remains remain, cased in concrete, fifty feet above ground, and now quite solid. (As one of my less tasteful companions put it, a rather stiff stiff. I did not reward his unseemly remark with even the ghost of a smile.)

Being sealed in a pillar of concrete, however, is the cause of the trouble I now find myself in. For, unfortunately, no one knows my earthly remains are there. No one, that is, who hasn't yet died. Worse still, no one knows I'm dead. Which is why my spiritual being is trapped here in this ghostly condition. As far as I can gather, one of the reasons, among many, why people get stuck between 'life' and 'after life' is that their deaths are unknown to their earthbound relatives.

(I was very surprised, I might tell you, to discover how many people get caught in this state of being, for all kinds of reasons. You expect to find murderers, of course, and there are plenty – though on the whole they turn out to be jolly nice blokes; but I was taken aback at the number of schoolteachers, for example, and politicians and army officers. The teachers and politicians spend most of their time trying to talk their way out into the 'after life', and never succeed. The army officers, however, take to this life very well. They enjoy going on what they call 'chill jaunts' – the kind of haunting that makes earthbound people scream and turn pale. I need hardly add they do this as badly as most of them did everything else in their earth life. Not that this matters much, for with its loss of popularity among earth people, ghostly haunting is rather a disappointing occupation these days. Everybody here is in very low spirits about it.)

But I'm rambling again. It's one of the hazards of being a ghost. You have so much time on your hands and very little to do with it.

As I say, being caught in the in-between, ghostly life – a kind of limbo-land between mortality and eternity – is a bit of a bore, and my aim is to pass on as quickly as possible. But to do this, my relatives must be informed of my death. And as they are not likely to discover my remains in their present secure location, the chances of my parents discovering my death are pretty slim. So I decided I must somehow or other get a message to them.

You have no idea how difficult it is to get a simple message from the 'dead' to the 'living'! The living just won't listen; and this present climate of disbelief in the after life only makes the task more difficult. I asked some of the older ghosts round here for advice. Everyone told me the same thing: don't bother. It would be a waste of time and energy, they said, and I'd only end up getting the jitters. I know now what they meant: talking to people who pretend you aren't there is worse than being sent to coventry. At least when people send you to coventry they don't pretend you aren't there; they just ignore you.

However, being a newcomer to the ghostly life, I refused to listen to such good advice. They were all old codgers, I told myself, spirits whose energies were worn out, sapped by years of failure. They had stopped trying ('given up the ghost' seemed hardly the right expression under the circumstances). What was wanted was a little enterprise, a little originality, and most of all, some determination. I believed

I possessed all three in quantity. My older companions smiled tolerantly, as wise old men always do when confronted with youthful foolishness, and drifted away to enjoy themselves at their leisure.

So, heedless of good counsel, I set to work. Two factors led to my first method of attempting to get in touch. First, though I wanted to communicate with my relatives, I did not want to upset them by suddenly materializing unannounced in the front room at home while they were watching television. They might have joined me in my present state, dispatched here by shock. Dad, after all, had a weak heart, and Mum has always been of a nervous disposition. I did think of contacting my girl-friend Veronica, who, in a way, was responsible for the situation I am now in. But she had already taken up with another fellow, and the one thing that was clear to me even then was that it is useless trying to make contact with mortals who have lost all interest in you, as well as having no belief in ghosts anyway. Veronica had certainly lost interest in me within a couple of days of my 'disappearance', as I knew from what I had observed of her evenings out with her new boy-friend (the one who was causing the trouble that started me thinking that led to me slipping into the concrete-mixer!). As for ghosts – Veronica went all through the film of *Nightmare House* without a twinge of fear, while it scared me for weeks. So Veronica was out!

The second thing that decided me on my first course of action was that, being a novice at materialization and ghostly activities in general, it was easier to appear at the place of my death than anywhere else. That meant a haunting of the mixing yard at work.

Fine, I thought; just right. I'll do my stuff in front of Harry, and I'll appear looking just as I did on the fatal day, dressed in my overalls. He'll be sure to recognize me then, and be less likely to get the willies, thinking he is seeing any old ghost.

With the confidence that ignorance inspires in men, I went through the materialization routine and successfully took my former shape three feet from Harry at four-thirty on the afternoon of the Thursday following the day I died. It was a beautiful day, the sun shining from a blue sky as it sank towards the spring evening. Harry was tending the mixer stripped down to his vest he was so warm.

I stood there in front of him for a full minute and more, waiting for him to catch sight of me. I nodded and smiled in a friendly way so that he would know I wasn't a malevolent type (we had, after all, had our arguments from time to time). He kept glancing at me, but showed not a flicker of reaction. At first this didn't bother me; he's a slow-witted lad. But then I started to lose patience. I waved at him, danced about a bit, even took a step nearer to him. He would have to be blind not to see me now, I thought.

Then I heard a cough at my elbow. I dematerialized to find an old ghost by the name of Cathcart Fitzgammon standing by my side. He was tut-tutting in a haughty manner, and shaking the grey-haired locks he insists on keeping so as to retain his eighteenth-century looks.

'Dash it, young feller,' he said. 'You'll do no good like that.'

I felt a bit bad-tempered that he had interrupted my very first haunt in such a way.

'Why not?' I snapped.

'Daylight haunts need considerable skill and experience, old chap,' he said. 'Besides which, you were standing with the setting sun right behind you. That poor mortal whose attention you hoped to attract would never have seen you,

no matter how bright you managed to make your appearance. You haven't a hope in . . . er . . . on Earth of catching his eye. If I were you I'd have a go during the night. It's easier then.'

He drifted off without another word, chuckling to himself.

Of course, I had to admit that Cathcart was right. He had also put me off my stroke, and I needed time to collect myself again. So I postponed operations for an hour or two while I considered the situation.

The difficulty was that if I appeared in daylight Harry would probably not see me, but if I waited until dark, or dusk even, Harry would have gone home, so that there would be no one to communicate with anyhow, and I'd be left shivering and alone in the cold.

As far as I could see, there was only one solution. I found Harry's car in the work's car-park, dissolved inside and made myself comfortable on the back seat, intending to wait until Harry knocked off work and went home. Then, when he went out for the evening, I'd materialize on the passenger seat beside him at a convenient moment and tell him my news. That way I'd know where Harry was when darkness fell, saving myself ohms of energy flying about looking for him.

Car-parks are dismal places, as much for ghosts as mortals – which is why you rarely hear of hauntings in them – and there was no one about of my kind to pass the time of day with; so very soon I was bored, and what with the bright sun and the stuffy warmth of Harry's car, I very soon dozed off. (There's nothing like bright light and warmth for setting a ghost nodding.) Half an hour after dissolving into Harry's car I was as dormant as a flat battery.

I came to hours later. Night had fallen, and was encouragingly black, without stars or Moon. It was so black, I thought at first the car must be parked in Harry's garage. But then I heard a noise from the front seat that indicated very clearly that we weren't in Harry's garage at all. I looked up and there was Harry, necking with his girl-friend, a shapely lass from the accounts office at work. We were parked under some trees in a lay-by just out of town.

Naturally, I felt a little uncomfortable. I'm not one of those ghosts who go round peeping at friends they've left behind, enjoying the sight of them in all kinds of situations both public and private. (Personally, I think that's as sick an occupation for a ghost as it is for a mortal.) But I'd spent a good deal of time and energy already keeping up with Harry so that I could get my message to him, and I wasn't going to give in now.

I had to act quickly, before things got really embarrassing. Without another thought I went through the drill for materialization at double-quick pace. Unfortunately, in my haste I put too much energy into some parts of the drill and not enough into others, and was rather careless overall. My lack of experience as a haunter, you see! The result was astonishing, and, but for the circumstances, might have been both interesting and amusing.

The materialization got completely out of control. Instead of appearing as myself in a gentle glow of unearthly light, I came out as a collection of very violent, phosphorescent colours revealing a hideous object with an enormous head, twisted features, a bloated body and unfinished, stunted arms and legs.

I did not realize at first just how I looked, for, of course, my attention was fully directed at Harry's back so that I should be ready to speak soothing words as soon as he turned round. So, thinking all was well, I coughed politely to attract his attention. But the cough also came out quite unlike what I intended. Instead of a soft, hacking noise, I heard myself produce what I can only describe as a cataract of prolonged and vicious snarls.

At once I knew that something was wrong, took a glance at myself, and immediately felt angry with myself for being so careless. Which only made matters worse. For my annoyance was transmitted into the materialization and imprinted itself on the warped features of the ghostly figure I had projected, turning an already ghastly face into something so horrible that I almost fainted at the sight of it.

The blaze of phosphor colours, the appearance of my misshapen ghost, the imprinting of my anger on its features: all happened in the blinking of an eye. But it was enough to attract Harry's and his girl's attention. They unravelled themselves with incredible speed, swung round in their seats, and came face to face with my apparition just as the snarls that were meant to be a cough broke the silence of the night.

For a split second they stared in wide-eyed disbelief at the appalling creature hovering in the air above the back seat. Stunned shock was replaced by nerve-shattered fear. The blood drained from their faces; their mouths dropped open. Then each one let out an hysterical scream.

This brought me to my senses. I dematerialized with such speed that the warped and shining figure I had created, instead of fading away, exploded like a searchlight bulb fusing from a short-circuit. The car was plunged into a blackness that seemed, by contrast with the brief brilliance of my ghostly glow, to be tangible.

I had no time to think how I might remedy my awful

error. Harry's girl flung open the car door and ran in blind terror screaming into the night. Harry was only a heartbeat behind.

They left me exhausted on the back seat.

It took me an hour to collect my thoughts and reorganize my energy, after which I felt so disappointed I trailed off home to my concrete pillar and stayed there for two days, suffering from acute depression.

Ghost friends told me I should have been more than pleased with myself. They pointed out, in their efforts to cheer me up, that in these days of disbelief in spectres I should be proud at my success in scaring two mortals out of their wits. But I'm afraid I couldn't see it like that. I had made a hash of the thing I really wanted to do; and I had been professionally careless. There was no excuse for such things. And as a result I was paying the price: I was still slopping round in ghostly limbo. Not that it is a bad life, as lives go. But it is not the ultimate . . . not the life any sane soul desires. And when you are within range of that life, as I am now that I am dead, the desire becomes a yearning almost painfully strong. The wise old man who said that Hell is the yearning to be in Heaven was right after all. But I cannot satisfy that yearning until I can persuade some mortal that I *am* dead, that my earthly remains are safely stowed away among the steel girders and concrete pillars of the Sure Shield Insurance Building, Manchester.

Two days' rest worked wonders. I got over my depression, recharged myself, did a good deal of thinking. The third day I spent discussing my new ideas with the most experienced ghosts who lived within convenient range of my billet in the pillar. The consensus of opinion was that I had two possible courses of action open to me. Neither was easy to pull off successfully.

I chose spirit possession first.

To get the best results from spirit possession you need an emotionally unstable mortal with a vivid imagination and a mind open to suggestion. All the experts told me that teenage girls are admirable for the purpose. And I knew just the right one for me. My sister.

Angela is sixteen. She is emotionally so unstable that she is as happy as a lark one minute and weeping like a sick willow the next. Her imagination is vivid to the point of being lurid (at any rate, it allows her to see pimply teenage boys as Greek gods, which anyone has to admit takes a powerful imagination). As for her mind, it is as pliant as warm plasticine. On the other hand, like most girls of her age, her constitution is as tough as tempered steel, so I had no fears of any ill effects on her health if my still rather amateur ghosting went badly wrong, as it had done with Harry. (Harry, by the way, recovered his car the next day in broad daylight, after which he had the local vicar exorcize it – something I regarded as extravagant cheek, seeing he never goes near a church from one year's end to the next.)

Angela would do nicely. She also had the added advantage of being one of the family; she would know who and what I was talking about without tiresome and lengthy explanations.

The only trouble was that possession takes a day or two to get going properly. Had I appreciated before I began how much hard work goes into it on the ghost's part, I'd certainly have dropped the entire idea at once. As it was, I went ahead with enthusiasm.

I gave the first night up to dream-making. Well before Angela's normal bedtime I settled myself in her room, and began to compose myself for the task ahead, inventing the dreams I'd put into Angela's head once I'd got inside her – a tricky business in itself. When her bedtime came, I was fully in the spirit of the occasion.

Angela's bedtime came, but Angela did not. She did not even arrive home from an evening out until twelve-thirty. By then my concentration was already a bit frayed; instead of feeling calm, collected and spiritually prepared, I was irritable, out of joint, and sparking all over the place with nasty thoughts about my sister. I recalled ruefully that this was exactly the effect Angela had usually had on me during our earthly life together.

When at last she arrived home, Dad was waiting to haul her over the coals for being out so late without permission. They argued. Angela flounced up to her room. By this time she was in no condition for me or anyone else to possess in any way at all. After slamming her door, she crashed round her room for quarter of an hour giving vent to her temper; then for ten minutes she wept soulfully on her bed just loudly enough for the parents to hear her but not so loud that either of them would come in and console her. Finally, she pulled off her clothes, threw them in a heap on the floor, and fell bad-tempered into bed, where she lay awake for ages inventing the most lurid and morbid fantasies I have yet encountered in anyone's mind, fantasies involving Dad, her boy-friend (who had kept her out late) and herself (in dramatic, romantic and, needless to add, tragic situations).

I could hardly summon up enough brotherly affection

and tenderness to go on with my plan. Indeed, for a while I was sorely tempted to give her the most blood-curdling, spine-chilling haunt I could manage, just to teach her a lesson. But eventually she drifted off to sleep and I pulled myself together and went to work.

You'll appreciate that, at this point, I must leave out technical details. The method by which one gets inside another person to control their thoughts is difficult enough to explain to a spirit; it is almost impossible to do so to a mortal. But should a mortal by some chance understand the explanation, then they would possess information that would give them a power over others of an extraordinary kind. If this power fell into the wrong hands you can see what evil could be let loose in the world.

All I can say is that for a couple of hours I gave Angela the treatment. I started out with pleasant memory dreams. I used one about the two of us years ago when she was still very small and I saved her from drowning in a seaside pool all of six inches deep. At least I told Mum I had saved her, and Angela was only too glad to take part in the deception because it sounded such a dramatic story and she was the centre of it. I used the one about the Christmas when she was thirteen and I gave her the first pair of nylons she had ever owned, along with a gigantic box of Swiss chocolates (a rather spiteful gift actually, as she was trying to slim at the time, being just at the puppy-fat age). Then I brought back the time when I stood up for her against Mum and Dad; Angela wanted to stay out late at a party for the first time in her life. (This seemed an appropriate memory to recall, considering the events of the night.)

There was lots more of this kind of thing before I decided

she had had enough. I juggled everything about, of course, and exaggerated bits here, suppressed unpleasant details there, and generally coloured the dreams so that everything was larger than life: a real potpourri of a dream, it was. By the time I was finished Angela was in a very receptive mood indeed, whimpering with nostalgia for the happy times we'd had together. (In fact, we were always bickering and back-biting; but time and dreams, and death most of all are powerful antidotes to people's recollections of the truth, as you'll have noticed, I expect.)

This done, I was ready to start on the big scene, a surrealist nightmare that Salvador Dali would have been proud to invent. Angela saw me in every deadly situation imaginable. I fell from a cliff into swirling, angry waves over which the sun shone, but a sun that looked like a huge illuminated clock with the hands showing three-thirty – the time at which I slipped into the mixer. I pictured her stirring a pan of porridge (she hates porridge); she saw an insect threshing about in the pan, looked closer, saw it was not an insect but me! At that moment I disappeared under the surface and the oven clock rang its alarm bell with the hands pointing to three and six. On and on, until Angela was in a sweat of anxiety and was beginning to suspect what I wanted her to: that I was dead, and not just 'missing'. In the end she was moaning, and shaking her head in her sleep, as if saying 'No, no!'

All this took a vast amount of energy, and I was soon dangerously tired. I decided that, before things got out of control, I should get some rest and observe the outcome of my first night's work. But, just to make sure that Angela did not dismiss her dreams when she woke up, I waited until the morning light brought her back to consciousness. Then, as soon as she opened her eyes, I picked up a bottle of cold cream from her dressing-table and hurled it across the room.

That did it. Angela was out of bed and into Mum's room without a second thought. There she poured out her confused dreams, confusing them all the more by trying to recount them to someone else. Mum thought Angela was ill; Dad as always listened calmly and said nothing. Angela insisted that her dreams were an omen, that I had not gone off somewhere secretly as everyone said, but that I had died somehow, and not very pleasantly. Mum burst into tears and told Angela not to talk like that. 'Where there's life there's hope,' she said. (I told you people no longer believe you're alive when you're dead!) Angela then burst into tears too, said no one ever had understood her but me, that she knew, just *knew*, her dreams meant that I was dead, and that she felt like running away and never coming back. Dad sighed deeply and got up, saying he felt like a nice cup of tea. After this, Angela stormed from the room, dressed hurriedly, and left for school without eating any breakfast or saying another word.

I had the uneasy feeling that my attempt to get a message to my family via Angela was doomed to failure. But I pressed on.

The next night I repeated the dreams, but this time I ended them by engraving a mental picture of myself in a tragic pose deep in Angela's mind before throwing a few things round the room in best poltergeist fashion just as she woke up.

Once again Angela ran to Mum. She was so desperately

convincing and distressed that Mum took her seriously, listening sympathetically to her story. Mum even came into Angela's room to see the mess I'd made. Dad went off at the first sign of trouble to make himself a cup of tea.

Angela, placated by Mum's sympathy and excited by the effect of her performance – she loves to be the central figure in a drama – set off for school in high spirits, and there recounted her tale to all and sundry, though only after swearing each person to secrecy and telling them it was all in the strictest confidence.

All that day I sat quietly smiling to myself; here was progress after all. Another night and I could reveal myself and the details of my death and departure.

The third night was much the same as the other two, with the addition of a ghostly and audible voice whispering '*Angela . . . Angela . . .*' before my sister dropped off to sleep, and a bout of sleepwalking before I dispossessed her in the morning. I had every hope of complete success.

My hopes were soon dashed.

Angela woke pale, fatigued and dizzy. I had overdone things.

Mum took one look at the limp figure in the bed and sent for a doctor. There was, of course, nothing seriously the matter with the girl. True, she was tired and running a temperature. But all she needed was a day's rest.

The situation now got out of control. The doctor was suspicious, though he pretended otherwise to Angela. He prescribed a tranquillizer and told her to stay in bed. But downstairs, he told Mum to 'keep an eye on that girl and report any change in her condition'. Mum was only too delighted to have an opportunity of mothering her only daughter and watched her every minute of the day and as much as she could manage of the following night.

Dad drank endless cups of tea.

Unimportant though these things may appear, they put me in a swivet. The tranquillizers made my task three times more difficult than before; my experience as a ghost was too limited to cope with the powers of modern medical science. Mum on the watch meant that if I tried a haunt she would be sure to see the effects, which would upset her more than I could bear. As for Dad's endless tea drinking: I recognized this as a sure sign that things were getting on top of him and I had even less desire to upset him than I had to upset Mum. If he started worrying, the strain might affect his dicky heart and for all I knew he'd end up joining me. This was a responsibility I dared not take.

For a day or two I let things ride, hoping Angela's health would improve, when I could start work again. But during the doctor's last visit, Mum had a long private chat with him, telling him all about Angela's dreams, and about the things being thrown round her room. The doctor said that he'd thought as much – he'd known at once that something was up. It was, he said, a common ailment among girls of Angela's age; the best thing would be to take Angela to a psychiatrist.

I dropped my plans like a hot brick there and then and fled back to my pillar in the insurance building. Psychiatrists were the last people I wanted to tangle with – or to tangle with my sister; they can make a haunting so complicated and mess one about so much that it just isn't worth the effort. (It doesn't surprise me one bit that this ghostly limboland is teeming with psychiatrists; more of them get stuck here than of any profession. And I've never heard of one of them getting through to the other side. Old Freud mopes around, muttering about sex, and Jung is always arguing with him and seeing archetypal patterns in the least likely places and events. They're a hopeless bunch!)

Well, my defeat at Mum's hands left me one more solution worth trying. Automatic writing. If this failed then I was condemned to a desultory life in this ghostly state for years – maybe centuries – until someone accidentally found my remains in the insurance building. Luckily, modern buildings are made to last no more than a few years, so my prospects of being discovered were brighter than those of ghosts whose bodies are buried in ancient buildings that were built to last for ever.

I consulted the experts once more. Having recovered their cool after the shock of hearing any ghost as inexperienced as myself announce that he was taking up automatic writing – something only the most advanced and knowledgeable haunters ever even contemplate – they gave me a lot of useful tips.

They warned me, for instance, not to employ professional mediums and clairvoyants. Professionals, they said, are usually phoney anyway and have never made contact with anything more than their instinct for making money at the expense of the credulous. And those who are genuine spirit contacts, born with the power to speak the words spirit people put into their minds, are just like all actors: they love to add and take away from the original script. Never satisfied to let the spirit work through them, they can't resist adding a touch of detail there, and missing the main point here;

while they have an insatiable taste for melodrama: for dressing up in weird clothes, and rigging outlandish gimmicks, and upstaging any poor spirit who is foolish enough to get involved with them. No, my advisers said, they are an odd lot and best left alone.

'What you must do,' they told me, 'is find an ordinary person who is clairvoyant and doesn't know it. They are the people most likely to have the special make-up of personality you need to work through, while they won't try to take part themselves in writing your message.'

I spent five weeks looking round for suitable mortals, ones with the right qualities for such difficult work as I had in mind: people pure in spirit, innocent in nature, neither naïve nor over-wise. Above all they must possess great faith, faith in life as worth living despite its horrors and troubles, faith in human nature and the durability of that incomparably beautiful but elusive creation, the human soul. Such people, I discovered, are rare indeed.

But I found one in the end, though with a little thought I might have realized where to look and searched here first. I came to this old people's home on the edge of town only this evening. A deaf old man lives here, and has done for the last twenty years since his wife died. He has two sons, both big men in business these days and very busy. Too busy ever to come and see the old man. He has a daughter too, but she has her own family to cope with and manages to visit only on special occasions like Christmas and her father's birthday.

So he passes his days alone, reading and thinking and watching the world go by in the silence of his being. For forty years he worked day in, day out as a joiner. He loved his garden, brought his family up as tenderly as he cared for his tomatoes and sweet peas. From his early twenties the pride and joy of his life was his beloved wife; and she doted on him as much as he on her – though she sometimes pretended otherwise. Now she is gone, he is too old to garden, his children are grown up and scattered. At first, after his wife's death, he grieved bitterly; but he conquered his grief, and every day that passes his faith deepens in the world to come.

This is the man who now writes this message for me. My hope is that, when he wakes and finds these hastily scribbled pages by his bedside, the pencil still clutched in his gnarled old hand, he will do me one further act of kindness, like the many others which have passed unnoticed in his life, and convey my news to my family. Or . . .

Perhaps not . . .

I begin to see that this old saint has something to teach me, who should be beyond teaching . . .

Perhaps, old man, it is best that my sudden end and my curious whereabouts remain unknown. Perhaps I need time to dwell as much as you have done on the nature of life and death. Perhaps when I have done this and plumbed the depths of that knowledge I will be ready to pass from this staging post of death into the life eternal – as ready as you are now to pass from mortality into immortality without a stopping place between.

Quite a thought!

Perhaps after all I am in this limboland for a purpose I had not understood. Till now.

I'm grateful to you, old man.

But I will leave this message by your side for your eyes

only to see. It can be a sign to you that you have not lived in vain. After reading it, do with it as you please.

Peace . . .

NOTE: *These papers were by the bedside of Mr James Henry Gibbons on the morning he was found dead, aged seventy-eight. I suppose they are the ramblings of a dying man's imagination.*

Signed: A. C. Harris, Warden, The Hermitage.

Also in Puffins

BOOK OF GHOSTS AND HAUNTINGS

Aidan Chambers

Ghosts are fascinating, but they are also frightening and it is reassuring to know that it is now possible to make a more scientific classification of different types of ghosts. They fall into four distinct groups: experimental, crisis, post-mortem and those ghosts who keep haunting the same place. In this book Aidan Chambers has gathered together a fascinating collection of material about each type, and has drawn extensively on the papers of the Society of Psychical Research. There are sections on spiritualism, the problems of photographing ghosts, mediums and séances, poltergeists, and a brief guide to some of the more interesting haunted houses of Great Britain and Ireland.

IT

William Mayne

Alice was in a mess that year. Her family had a low opinion of her because she was dreamy and spoke out of turn. Her brother had passed into the choir school, but she had failed the entrance exam to hers. So she was in a wilderness, the wrong way out for everybody else. But then odd things started happening when Alice was around: poltergeist tricks, sudden winds, eggs breaking themselves. Her friend Raddy was exasperated. 'Are you training for a witch?' she asked. But Alice just grew more brooding, absorbed in this strange restless being that was going around with her – until finally she understood what IT wanted and could do something about it.

GHOSTLY GALLERY

Alfred Hitchcock

Ten weird and uncanny ghost stories collected by the master of mystery. They include really spooky, spinechilling stories, some fanciful ones, and some where the phantoms and apparitions are even treated humorously. Some of them are true shades of darkness and others, stranger still, appear in the glare of the sun at noon or deep in the forest shadows – you may see a spook any day of your life. For fearless readers of ten upwards.

THE SHADOW-CAGE AND OTHER TALES OF THE SUPERNATURAL

Philippa Pearce

Quite ordinary things turn out to be haunted in the world Philippa Pearce creates – a funny little statue, an old biscuit barrel, a nursery cupboard – and in quite ordinary circumstances. Memories of past unhappiness can cling to a place connected with them. A man out for his evening exercise can find his hatred of his brother suddenly taking shape as a running companion. And human passions can even reach beyond the grave if they're powerful enough – a mother's longing for her daughter's return, an old man desperate at the neglect of his once-cherished garden. These ten stories are written with all the fine perception for which their author is celebrated.

THE WATCH HOUSE

Robert Westall

'Those rocks?' asked Anne. 'They don't look dangerous!' But there was a spooky feeling to the lifeboatman's watch house on the cliff above. There were bound to be ghosts in a place so stuffed with relics of violent, unhappy deaths at sea. This is a gripping ghost story for older readers by the author of the Carnegie Medal winner, *The Machine-Gunners.*

THE SHADOW GUESTS

Joan Aiken

The deep mystery surrounding the disappearance of Cosmo's mother and elder brother had never been solved. Then peculiar things began to happen to Cosmo at the old mill house where he was staying. Strangers appeared and only Cosmo could see them. What did they want? Where, or *when*, did they come from?

UNDER THE MOUNTAIN

Maurice Gee

Apart from having red hair, there is nothing remarkable about the Matheson twins. Or so they think. Imagine their horror, then, when they discover that only they can save the world from dominance by strange, powerful creatures who are waking from a spellbound sleep of thousands of years . .

PSSST